Destiny

CHAS WILLIAMSON
A South Mountain Journey of Faith: Book 1

Copyright © 2023 Chas Williamson
All Rights Reserved

Print ISBN:978-1-64649-311-1
eBook ISBN:978-1-64649-312-8
Large Print:978-1-64649-313-5

Year of the Book
135 Glen Avenue
Glen Rock, PA 17327

This is a work of fiction. Names, characters, businesses, places, events and incidents are either the products of the author's imagination or used in a fictitious manner. Any resemblance to actual persons, living or dead, or actual events is purely coincidental.

Prelude

Selena delighted in the sweet scent of the corsage. The flower even smelled cold, as if it had just been picked with the cool morning dew still heavy on its petals. But the beauty of the adornment couldn't compare with the sight of the man standing before her. Trey's eyebrows raised slightly before shifting into a wink. "Would you like me to pin this on you?"

John, Selena's father, answered instead. "I'll do it." With a Marlboro clenched between his lips, the older man's hands trembled as he attached the decoration to Selena's dress. John took a step back and then snuffed the cigarette in an ashtray. Despite his tough expression, Selena detected the drop of moisture at the corner of his eye.

"Thank you, Daddy."

"Girl, you look more and more like your mother every day. She was the prettiest woman I've ever seen, 'cepting maybe you." His eyes were now glistening. He sniffed hard before adding, "Be right back. Need to go find the camera."

When John left the room, Trey stepped forward and took Selena's hands. "Your dad's right. You are the most beautiful girl in the entire universe. Thanks for going to the prom with me."

"Who else would I go with?" After all, they'd been dating since tenth grade. "You and me, we belong together."

"That we do." He was so handsome, standing there taking her in. Trey wore his hair longer than most kids, but made sure every single strand was in place. The normal shadow of whiskers was missing from his chin and cheeks tonight. Trey looked like he'd stepped from the cover of a magazine. But Selena noticed something troubling in those blue eyes.

"Everything okay?"

Trey hesitated. "Yeah, well, we need to talk later."

"About what?"

"It's not important right now. I want us to enjoy the dance."

Before Selena could respond, her father returned. "Took me a while to find this thing." John held up the old SLR camera that had once belonged to Selena's mother. "As soon as I thread the roll of film in here, I'll be ready. Let's head outside."

Selena reached for Trey's hand and led the way out the door. Her boyfriend's fingers were trembling. It took her father a few minutes to find just the right setting. They decided not to use the red brick of the apartment building as a background, but instead walked across the street to a neighbor's flower garden. It seemed her dad was taking longer than usual to snap the photos. When John was finished, they returned to the apartment door. Her father removed the pack of cigarettes from his pocket and stuck one between his lips. He held a lighter in his left hand.

Tray glanced at his cell. "Our reservations at the Log Cabin are in thirty minutes. We need to leave soon."

"Don't let me hold you up." John pulled the stick of tobacco from his lip before he turned to Selena. He drew her into a tight embrace and then whispered in her ear, "I'm so proud of you. Have fun tonight."

"Thanks. Love you too, Daddy."

Trey held the door to his mother's old Impala for Selena and then climbed into the driver's seat. He was quiet as he pointed the vehicle in the direction of Leola.

"Something's on your mind. What's going on?"

"It's been a bad day."

"What happened?"

His lips were quivering and when he spoke, his voice was higher than normal. "I've told you about the arguments between my parents. It reached a boiling point at breakfast and after a world class screaming match, they decided to call it quits. Dad moved out this morning."

The relationship of Trey's parents had been strained for quite a while.

"I'm so sorry. Where did he go?"

Trey's eyes narrowed. "He said he was going to move in with one of his fellow students... the one my mom calls his 'college girlfriend'. She's about our age."

"Tell me how you're feeling."

"No. It will take too long."

"Then, let's skip the dance and find someplace to talk."

Her boyfriend shook his head. "Thank you, but not tonight. There's only one senior prom and I want those memories to be about you, not them."

Selena rubbed his arm. "It's up to you, but if you change your mind... I hope you know how much I love you. I always will."

A smile again appeared on his face. "That's one thing I'll never forget."

***

Graduation had come and passed. Selena was sitting on her bed, contemplating what she needed to pack for college. Following in the footsteps of her mother, she had decided to become a nurse. Offered an Army ROTC scholarship, Selena was heading off to the University of North Carolina. Trey had also committed to the same school, getting a partial ride for football.

The hardest part would be leaving her father. As a long-distance trucker, Selena was used to his frequent absences. Her grandparents and neighbors had often watched her while he was on the road. But something nagged her. What concerned her most was the increased amount of hacking when he got up in the morning. The two pack a day habit was darkening his future. Selena suspected his cigarette consumption had increased tremendously as her departure approached. The dirty habit was his coping mechanism.

The shrill ring of the cell derailed her train of thought. Selena smiled when she glanced at the screen. "Hey, Trey. How are you?"

"Not so good. Got a couple of minutes?"

"Sure. What's going on?"

"I'm outside. Can we do this face to face?"

Face to face? "Uh, sure."

Without another word, he disconnected. She felt bad that Trey's home situation was so tough. After his dad walked out, Trey had tried to step up and help his mom with the yard work, cooking, cleaning and taking care of his three younger siblings. Selena made every effort to be the bright spot in his life.

Trey was sitting on the hood of his mother's Chevy when she stepped outside. She noticed how his eyes didn't quite meet hers when she approached.

"Hi, babe. What's up?"

"I, uh, I've got some bad news."

Selena brushed the hair from his eyes. "Whatever it is, we'll get through it together."

He rubbed his hand over his mouth and chin before again speaking. "I decided I'm not going to college."

***

Trey had practiced this speech for days, but now that the time was here, he struggled with the words. How he wished things could be different, but his topmost concern was the well-being of the girl he loved.

Selena's face was pale. "Why aren't you going? If it's the money, I've got some saved up. It's yours."

Compassion ran in her veins, always caring more about others than herself. "Yes, it's the money... and my mom... and my sisters. Mom can't make ends meet anymore. I need to help her out."

"Isn't your dad contributing?"

The air was stifling. "You know Dad was a grad student. Mom is the bread winner. Because he has very little income, she will have to pay *him* alimony or offer a settlement. It looks like Mom might have to sell the house to buy him out."

It was plain to see Selena was furious. "She needs to get a lawyer."

"Mom has a good one, but I think maybe Dad's is much better."

Selena's lips were white where she had them clamped together. "This isn't right. Excuse me for saying this, but that man's a jerk. Doesn't he realize how he's affecting your future?"

"Dad could care less. All he worries about is getting his doctorate and being with that little honey he's living with."

"Then what are you going to do?"

"I took a job with a plumber as an apprentice. I have a duty to help out the family. It doesn't pay a lot now, but I think it will be a good choice in the long run."

It was easy to see the kindness in her face. "Then no to college, for now. Okay, you're postponing higher education for a while, but not permanently. Just don't give up your dreams."

Giving up a lot more than that. Trey waited until the pause was painful. "That may take years." He wiped his arm across his face. "I can't expect you to delay your life and your future while you wait for me."

"What? You are my destiny. Don't you realize that? I'll wait for you—even if it takes forever." She grasped and then squeezed his hands. "You and me, we were meant to be."

This was it, the moment he'd been dreading. "We both want that, but let's face the facts. It's over. I'm letting you go."

"Trey, you're not thinking straight."

"I am. I've been through this a million times, with my mom, my grandparents and even the pastor. You've got college and then the Army. Who knows where you'll end up being stationed? I'm not going to stand in the way of your life... or happiness."

"Don't you understand? *You* are my joy, my delight, my happiness. We'll figure a way out of this. Don't make a hasty decision you'll end up regretting. Let's talk about this."

Trey softly removed his hands from her grip. "There's nothing else to discuss. I've already made my decision. This is goodbye."

Selena's expression was one of shock. "Just like that? You're throwing us away because of what your dad did?"

"Don't make this tougher on me than it is. I have no other option."

"You always have a choice. Talk to me. We can work through this together."

Wish we could. But there was nothing else he could do. "No, it's over and done. I've got to go."

Selena's cheeks were wet. She shook her head and stared at him as if in disbelief. "Your mind is made up and this is what you really want to do?"

"It's not what I want to do. It's what I *need* to do."

The girl shuddered and then turned away. Selena paused and shot him another glance. "Then I guess this is goodbye. Have a nice life."

His gaze followed her until she disappeared into the apartment. The closing of the front door reminded him of a rock being rolled in front of a grave—his tomb. Trey's words were but a whisper. "Farewell, Selena. You'll forget me in time, but I'll love you—forever."

Chapter One

Ten Years Later

Beth Warren glanced at the screen. As the innkeeper of the Paradise Bed and Breakfast, there were two facts about her life—first, privacy was a cherished commodity, and second, time was never really her own. The guests always came first, meaning well-prepared breakfasts each morning, an immaculately clean inn every day and availability to the guests at all hours of the day and night. Take this evening for example. Beth and her husband Anderson wanted to take a drive over to neighboring York County to hike on the Rail Trail. Anderson loved trains, so this excursion would be to visit the Howard Tunnel—one of the oldest active train tunnels in America. But business had to come first. One guest was due to arrive sometime that evening, a Captain S. Harper. Beth had to greet the soldier before they could leave.

"Harper, Harper. Hmm, that name sounds familiar." Glancing at the information provided by the guest, the driver's license had been issued in Hawaii. No first name, only an initial. "Don't believe I know anyone from that state, anyway." Nothing else about the name immediately came to mind, so she dropped the thought and walked to the kitchen. Earlier, she'd set out salmon to thaw for supper. Her spouse would soon be home, and Beth wanted to have a hot meal waiting for him.

After starting the broiler, Beth's mind drifted to the man who shared her life. *Thank You, God, for my husband.* Anderson's smile filled her thoughts until she heard the front door open. Drying her hands, Beth stepped into the hallway. Movement to her left drew her attention. A medium height female soldier was standing in the large living room, admiring the huge stone fireplace and the photos on the mantle. The woman was wearing a dress uniform, consisting of a full-length skirt and jacket. A female officer's cap was on the table. Twin bars of a captain's rank adorned the shoulder of her coat.

Before Beth could speak, the lady reached up, grasped and removed a photo from the mantle—one of Beth and Anderson on their wedding day.

There was something peculiar about the way this person handled the picture. The woman's fingers outlined Beth's image. Surprisingly, Beth detected a soft sob before the frame was returned to the mantle.

"That was a special day, when Andy and I wed."

The soldier turned around. Beth took in the medical insignia on the collar and the nameplate that read, Harper. The lady had light brown hair that was trimmed short, reaching for but not touching the shirt's collar. There was something vaguely familiar. The woman stepped toward Beth.

"Beth? Beth Rutledge? Is that really you?"

"It is, or was. My last name is Warren now. Do I know you?"

"Selena Harper. We were neighbors for a while, until your mom married that young man."

The memories came flooding back. It was Beth's first year in Lancaster. Selena and her dad had been neighbors in the complex where her mom rented a small apartment. Those weren't happy times for Beth, until she and Selena met. The two had become inseparable BFFs. That changed after her mom married Sam and moved the family to the outskirts of Strasburg. Beth was suddenly sad that they'd drifted apart.

Selena's voice broke the trance. "Do you remember me?"

"Of course, I do." Beth hugged the lady. "How have you been? I see you're a captain in the Army."

"Yes, I am and I'm doing okay. What about you? I looked at the photo of you... in a wedding dress. I can't believe you're married."

"Yes. God brought me a wonderful man to share my life. Let's go into the kitchen. I'll brew us some tea and we can catch up while I make dinner."

Beth detected the deflated smile on her friend's lips. Selena was silent when Beth placed a cup of fragrant hibiscus tea on the table. "What brings you back to Lancaster?"

The soldier added sugar-free sweetener and cream to the brew. "I wanted to stop by to see my grandparents. Grandpop has dementia, but my grandmom's still getting around. They live in a senior facility near Millersville."

"How's your dad?"

Pausing to press a napkin to her lips before replying, Selena continued. "Dad died six years ago. Forty years of heavy smoking finally did him in. He lived just long enough to see my college graduation."

Things got a little blurry for a second or two. "I'm really sorry. I always liked your dad. I remember how he would give you bearhugs and call you his baby girl."

The soldier's eyes were also wet. "He was a great man. Worked hard all his life so I could have an easier future."

An uncomfortable silence followed until Selena spoke again. "What about your family? I loved your mom and secretly wished she and my dad would get together. Would have been nice to have her as my mother... and you as my sister. Are she and that man still married?"

"Absolutely. They're a shining example of true love." After a sip of tea, Beth continued. "Mom and Sam are doing quite well. They still live in the same place outside of Strasburg. Mom built a bakery next to the house. Since you last saw them, I have three more siblings—two sisters and a brother. Do you remember my little sister, Missi?"

"I do. We used to call her your shadow."

The memory brought a smile to Beth's face. "Wow, that was appropriate. She seems to be following in my footsteps. Missi's away at school right now, but will return in the fall. She plans to do long-distance learning to finish her degree in hospitality and tourism. Andy and I are hoping she'll take over my job."

"What would you do if that happens?"

"Since we want to start a family, I was thinking about going into some sort of business, maybe selling a unique type of craft or making jams. Who knows, could be I'll follow in Mom's footsteps and open a small bakery."

That comment brought a smile. "Your mom could really cook. I remember that tasty coconut cake with the three different kinds of chocolate icing she'd make. Goodness gracious. My mouth's watering just thinking about it."

"I'll ask her to whip one up for you." Beth glanced at the wall clock. "Andy will be home shortly. Would you like to join us for dinner?"

"No, I don't want to disturb your family time."

Beth touched her hand. "Just because my mom didn't marry your dad doesn't mean we're not family. In my heart, you'll always be my sister."

***

While Beth prepared the meal, Selena organized her room and then freshened up. The B&B had a very homey feel, unlike the sterile place she was used to living in. It was quite strange that she'd ended up here, and had run into Beth again. Perhaps God was answering Selena's prayer to re-direct her life. He had to know how badly she needed help.

Drifting back in time, Selena reflected on the close friendship she and the younger woman had shared. Just before they'd met, her father had relocated them to Lancaster from Harrisburg. Beth's mother had just moved in and the two girls struck up a wonderful friendship. That all changed when Beth's mom married and moved her family a couple of miles down the road. But distance wasn't the reason the friendship slackened. The real cause was because that Selena had met and quickly fallen in love with Trey Brubaker.

Descending the stairs, the luscious scent of broiled fish beckoned. Selena noted that the folding doors to the kitchen were closed. Beth had explained the reason she and her husband did that was to have privacy during their meals. Despite being instructed to just walk in, Selena knocked. A tall, muscular man with curly brown hair and steel blue eyes opened the door.

A smile immediately covered his face. "You must be Selena. Beth told me all about you. I'm her husband, Anderson, but you can call me Andy."

His handshake was firm but not overpowering. "It's a pleasure to meet you... Andy. Beth told me you're a geologist. What kind of work do you do?"

"I'm a regional manager for an environmental firm. That means I spend most of my days on the road, but thankfully I get to come home to my beautiful wife every evening."

Beth was working on the other side of the counter. The married woman quickly carried plates of food to the table. "I hope you're hungry. Tonight, we're having the bounty of the season to go along with the salmon steaks—broiled zucchini and baby carrots, and a fresh garden salad. For dessert, I prepared chilled strawberry soup."

The delectable aroma made Selena's mouth water. Anderson stood and helped his wife with her chair. The joy and happiness on Beth's face couldn't be missed. *Wish I had a love like that.* Glancing at the plate and the presentation, Selena couldn't help but giggle.

It must have been contagious because Beth joined her in laughter. "What's so funny?"

It was comforting being back in Lancaster, eating dinner with an old friend. *You knew I needed this. Thank You, Lord.* "You inherited the food gene from your mom, didn't you?"

Raising an eyebrow, Anderson asked, "What do you mean?"

"Maybe she's not like that anymore, but Beth's mom was always so trim despite the scrumptious food she'd make. And even if we were only having toasted cheese sandwiches, Hannah's preparation made me feel like I was in a five-star restaurant."

The man nodded. "Yep, my mother-in-law is still skinny and quite pretty, just like my wife. Must be hereditary. I have to work out almost an hour a day to keep from getting pudgy. But you are right, I married a master chef."

Beth's cheeks were pink as she shook her head. "Okay you two, please stop. Let's eat while the food's still warm. Andy, would you mind?"

Anderson bowed his head and reached for the hands of the two women. It had been a long time since Selena had joined hands with anyone in prayer. "Father, we thank You for the food we are about to partake and ask a special blessing on the hands that prepared it. We are grateful for friends, old and new, who are with us this evening. We pray for You to guide our footsteps and show us the path You intend for us. And thank You, Lord, for my wife. Amen."

Beth quickly replied, "And for my husband."

Passing the salad bowl to Selena, Andy spoke. "Beth tells me you're a nurse in the Army. What's that like?"

"I've had a couple of different duty stations. After graduation, I ended up in Virginia for a couple of months before being transferred to Germany, then Korea and finally Tripler Army Medical Center outside of Honolulu."

Beth wiped her mouth and then smiled broadly. "Andy and I honeymooned in Hawaii. His grandparents surprised us with a three-week trip as our wedding present. Of the four islands we visited, I enjoyed Oahu the most. The mountains and beaches were beautiful. Did you know there's actually a rainforest in Honolulu?"

"Yes. The Lyon Arboretum is part of the University of Hawaii. I've hiked their trails many times. Oahu is a great place to live."

"It's not like being on the islands, but Andy and I were planning on taking a jaunt on the Rail Trail in York County after dinner. Care to join us?"

"I wouldn't want to impose."

Andy added a second helping of salad to his plate. "Nonsense. We'd love to have you come along. There's this ice cream place over there called Mack's. It seems we always stop there on the way back."

Selena snickered. "How curious. You eat healthy, exercise and then indulge on frivolous calories?"

Beth also laughed. "That's life in Paradise."

After the meal, Beth quickly cleaned up while Selena changed into comfortable shoes, camo pants and a shirt with "Army Nurse Corps" emblazoned across the front. The three piled into an old red Explorer for the journey. Beth took the back roads and ended up catching Route 30 from the Old Philadelphia Pike.

"This area has really been built up since I left."

From the driver's seat, Beth responded. "I know. So much farmland is gone. Progress, I guess, but I, for one, think we have enough strip malls and high-density housing."

Anderson now chimed in. "That's one of the main reasons we're thinking about moving."

"Where would you go?"

Selena noted the quick glance between the married couple. Almost as one, they answered, "Gettysburg."

"The site of the Civil War battle, if I recall. Dad took me there once. But isn't that a tourist area, too?"

She could see Beth's expression in the rearview mirror. "Yep, big time. But we were thinking about settling a little north of town. Maybe in Biglerville or the Arendtsville area."

The driver's expression changed. "Look out your window. There's the Columbia bridge."

Many years had gone by since Selena had crossed the Susquehanna River. In that time, her perspective had changed. As a kid, she could have cared less about roads, but now the beautiful Art Deco bridge had an unsettling beauty. Selena's words almost caught in her throat. "Remember how my dad would call me when he was headed home and took in that sight? He used to say it was the gateway to paradise." *Miss you so much, Daddy.*

A silence between the three adults in the car followed. The voice of Kimberly Perry filled the quietness with music. Beth was playing an old Band Perry CD. Selena barely listened. Her thoughts were on not only the past, but the uncertain future awaiting her.

Almost thirty minutes later, Beth parked her Explorer in a small lot. Shadows were beginning to lengthen as they stepped onto the parking lot at Brillhart Station, just south of York.

Chipper as ever, Beth chattered away as they walked along what was once the Maryland and Pennsylvania railroad line between York and Baltimore. "The Howard Tunnel is a mile or so in front of us. Andy loves trains. Did I tell you where he proposed to me?"

"No."

"On the Strasburg Railroad. And to make sure I'd say yes, he did it in front of most of my friends and relatives. He and my mom conspired to..."

Her friend continued, but Beth's voice faded into the background. Selena's mind drifted back in time... to a point when happily-ever-after appeared to be within her reach. Not for the first time, Trey's face filled her mind. *Do you ever think of me?* The late summer day when he broke up with Selena had been the last time she'd seen or heard from him. *Do you ever wish...*

Anderson's voice snapped Selena out of the sentimental trip. The man was speaking to his wife.

"That's the Codorus Creek. It flows into the Susquehanna River a little northeast of York."

Beth turned and then smiled at her. "What do you think of the hike?"

"It's beautiful scenery."

"But not nearly as pretty as the tropics. Probably can't wait to go back to Hawaii, huh?"

Time to tell them the truth. "I'm not sure I'll be staying in Hawaii much longer."

Beth stopped and turned to face her. "Oh, no. Where's the Army sending you now?"

Selena took a deep breath before responding. "Out to pasture."

Chapter Two

The smile on the blonde's face lit up the room as soon as he entered. "Good morning. I brought you a cup of coffee and two of your favorite doughnuts."

Trey reached into a pocket for his wallet. "How much was the bill?"

Rose laughed and then shook her head. "Friends treat each other without any expectation in return. You owe me nothing. Today was my turn."

"Thanks."

"No problem." The beauty hesitated before continuing. "But... if you really want to return the favor, I'm free this weekend. There's an art festival in Havre de Grace. I'd love to watch the sun set from the boardwalk with you."

Her offer took him completely by surprise. "Uh, I don't know. Let's see how things play out." With his hand on the doorknob to the shop, he again glanced in Rose's direction. The girl was drop dead gorgeous. "Talk to you later. We're down three plumbers, so I'm heading out in the field today. Bye."

The sad smile and weak words of parting cut into him. Rose Sheppard was a very beautiful lady.

Kind, sweet, and wholly devoted to him. Trey couldn't think of a single negative trait the girl possessed... except that he was her boss.

The shop was empty as he headed for the service desk. Summer vacations had cut into his work force this week. Both Trey and his service manager, Reed Thomas, were on the road trying to hold down the fort. Best friends since childhood, Reed managed the skilled help, supplies and assignments while Trey did estimates and customer service.

Grabbing the keys for the trade van and an electronic work tablet, Trey stepped into the bright sunshine. After performing a safety check on the vehicle, Trey reviewed the work schedule. His first assignment would be a water heater replacement in Nottingham, then a stop in Quarryville to install a water softening system. The final job of the day would be in Paradise to upgrade the plumbing fixtures at the bed and breakfast. Ever efficient, Reed had already packed the supplies in the van.

The trill of Trey's cell caught his attention. "Hey, Mom. How are you this morning?"

"Not very well. My car won't start."

"Can you call Triple-A?"

"I can't wait for them to get out here. I'll be late, again."

It was probably the battery. Trey had encouraged his mother to replace her ancient Impala with a new car, even offering to pay for it. But he knew his mother well enough to know she wouldn't do it without his help. Since his father had left, Trey had become his mother's de facto life partner. "Let me see what I can do."

"Why can't you just take me to work?"

Her townhouse was in Ronks. If he picked her up and drove her to the job, he'd be an hour or so late for his appointment. "We're short this week, so I'm playing plumber."

"Okay, fine. Guess I'll just call for the tow truck and take my chances on not getting fired."

If nothing else, his mother had refined her ability to dole out guilt trips to a 'T'. "Hang tight. I'll have to juggle things around a bit, but let me see what I can do."

"Please hurry. I want to stop and grab a breakfast sandwich before I get there. There's absolutely nothing to eat in this house."

After disconnecting, he pulled over. There was another option, but Trey knew he was playing with fire. He briefly contemplated the situation before making the call.

Rose answered on the first ring. "Hey there. Did you miss me?"

"Uh, I guess so."

"What's up?"

"My mom's car broke down. Would you mind picking her up and taking her to work?"

There was a laugh in Rose's reply. "Of course not. You do realize that, for you, I'd do anything."

Trey knew Rose meant what she said, but not in a weird way. The girl was genuinely special. Not sure whether it was his conscience or heart that moved him, he blurted out, "As a thank you, how about dinner and that art show on Saturday?"

Silence greeted him. Rose's voice was whisper quiet. "Trey, you're not indebted to me. I was just teasing you earlier."

"I know, but—"

"This may seem forward, but I need to say it. I want to be wanted for me... not for what I can do for you. If that makes a difference in your offer, I understand."

Rose gave me an easy out. Should I take it? His mind drifted back to another girl... one he'd known a million years ago. One he'd been stupid enough to let go. *Not letting history repeat itself.*

"Still there?"

"Yes. Well, whether or not you act as a chauffeur for my mom, I am still asking you out. But please, let's keep it quiet at work, for both our sakes."

The happiness returned to Rose's voice. "I can't wait. I've been dreaming about this for two years. Gotta go. Your mom needs me to pick her up."

"Thanks, Rose."

Dropping the cell to the seat, Trey took a moment. The last time he'd been on a real date had been in high school. The face of that girl appeared before him, but her beautiful smile slowly turned to sadness, a stark reminder of the day they'd broken up, when happiness slipped from his life. Rose's beautiful visage appeared and slowly replaced the previous one. *Maybe it's really time to start living.*

***

Selena opened the book and made herself comfortable in the swing. She was sitting in the picturesque side garden of the B&B. On the porch,

Beth worked on clearing the breakfast dishes from the tables. In the backyard of the house next door, teenaged boys were playing baseball. A petite blonde child walked out of the home, followed by a short, beautiful blonde lady. Selena immediately recognized the woman as Sophie Miller, who owned the tea room down the road. That was where Trey had taken her on their first date. Selena's mind wandered back in time.

"What do you have planned for the day?" Beth stood in front of Selena, looking almost comical wearing a pair of cheap, red sunglasses and an oversized, floppy white hat.

How long was I daydreaming? "Nothing, really. I was going to relax and do some reading. What about you?"

"I'm heading up to Shady Maple Farm Market. Andy loves those rice cakes they make. Want to tag along? Maybe we can do an early lunch at the Smorgasbord. On the way back, I was going to stop at my mom's bakery. She made that special cake you love and I'm positive she wants to see you. The only thing is that I need to be back by two. I have a contractor coming to do some upgrades."

It was as if time between them had vanished and their friendship picked up from where they'd left off... as if they were still best friends... like they'd been years ago. "Sounds great. I'm going to take my grandmother out for an early dinner, so if we're back by two, I'll have plenty of time. Just give me five minutes to go get changed."

In less than half an hour, Beth eased her Explorer into a space at the Shady Maple complex.

Selena couldn't believe the number of buggies they'd seen. "I'd forgotten about the Amish. Seems like they're out in full force today."

Beth giggled, but then again, her young friend always appeared full of merriment. "They are really nice people. I'm going to miss them when we move."

Selena had never been inside this store before. The displays of fresh fruit and vegetables made her mouth water. "Why are you leaving the area?"

"Lancaster is becoming too populated, over busy. Andy and I want our lives to be slower paced... you know, like ours used to be."

"But why move to Gettysburg? You're just going from one tourist area to another."

"We're actually looking to buy a bit further north. We love to hike. The Appalachian Trail goes through Caledonia State Park. That was where Andy first told me he'd fallen in love with me."

Selena was quiet as they checked out at the market cashier and together walked up the hill to the Shady Maple Smorgasbord building. The delightful scent of steaks cooking on a grill made Selena's mouth water. It was difficult choosing wisely. Her plate was mostly filled with salad and veggies, though a small New York strip and a spoonful of roast beef were snuggled amidst the romaine. Beth, on the other hand, had heaped her platter with noodles, mashed potatoes, fried shrimp, fried chicken, cheese and a bagel slathered in cream cheese.

Selena chortled. "This isn't fair. I run five miles a day and watch what I eat in the struggle to stay trim."

"I just have lucky genes. Even when Mom was carrying my brother and sisters, she wasn't heavy."

"You two are really close, aren't you?"

Beth waited to respond until she'd finished chewing a mouthful of buttered noodles. "After Andy, Mom's my best friend. Always encouraged me. Pushed me to be the best version of myself I could be. Taught me more than how to cook or bake, but rather how to be loving and kind. Because of her, I believe I'm making a positive influence on others in my life."

Just how my mom would have been... if she were still alive. "Won't it be hard, moving away?"

Beth's expression clouded. "She and I have spoken about what's coming many times. We'll find a way to stay close, whether it's visits a couple of times a week or daily phone calls. I am who I am because of her and I'll never forget that."

Poking a cherry tomato with her fork, Selena looked away. "I wish I would have known my mother better. She died when I was four."

The warmth of her friend's hand over hers startled Selena. "I'm sorry. I know you told me, but I forgot. What happened?"

She had to sniff. "Mom was an Army ROTC nurse, just like me. She did twelve years of active duty before transferring to the reserves. She met and married Dad. Two years later, I was born. The first few years were wonderful. I remember we lived down south and went to the beach all the time. Then her unit got called up. They deployed to Iraq. On the way to a field hospital, a roadside IED wiped out her

Humvee. Mom and three other soldiers didn't make it."

"I'm so sorry."

Selena glanced at Beth, noting the moisture on her friend's cheeks. "The thing I remember most about Mom was how she smelled... like fresh roses. And her hair, so long and soft. She used to read to me before I fell asleep. I'd run my fingers through her mane and pretend she was Rapunzel."

They ate quietly in silence. "You're very lucky to be so close with your mom. Maybe you should reconsider moving."

Her friend shook her head. "We want to start a family. Lord knows we can't have one with my job."

"How soon are you planning to have children?"

"Hopefully in the next year or so. I know my sister Missi wants to fill my shoes at the B&B, so that's one reason we've stayed."

Selena used a knife to corral the last of the roast beef on her fork. "Are there other reasons?"

"Two, really. Running the bed and breakfast has its benefits. Like, not having to pay rent. Andy and I have socked away as much money as possible over the last five years. Housing prices in Adams County are lower than here, so we should have either a hefty down payment or maybe enough to buy a house outright."

"Holy cow. That's great." Selena noted the look of sorrow on Beth's face. "What's wrong?"

"The other reason I've stayed this long is because of Ellie Campbell."

"The name sounds familiar. Do I know her?"

"She and her husband Henry own Campbell Farms as well as the Bed and Breakfast. The building actually used to be their home, but Ellie's vision gave the place a new chapter in its rich history."

The sip of iced tea helped wash down Selena's meal. "Must be a great boss. Why would you stay for her?"

Beth wiped her cheeks. "Ellie and Henry have been like a second set of parents to me. I can't let her down."

"Okay. What does that mean?"

"Ellie's been sick for the last several years."

Despair suddenly infiltrated the room. "How sick?"

"She almost died. Ellie has cancer."

***

"I am absolutely stuffed." *Understatement of the year.* Selena was about to burst at the seams. They were driving back from Hannah's Bakery in Strasburg. "That cake was somehow even better than I remember. I must have gained twelve pounds today."

Giggling, Beth teased her. "Feel free to join Andy and I on our evening hike."

"Are you going back to York County?"

"No. We plan on picking up the Mount Gretna trail just above Elizabethtown. Our reward will be getting a sundae at the Jigger Shop."

"I swear. You know, those high-calorie foods will one day come back to haunt you."

"Maybe, but for now, your jealousy is showing. Have you ever been there? I mean Mount Gretna?"

Trey took me there, long ago. "I was there once to see a show at the Playhouse. Daddy also took me there a couple of times for ice cream."

"Then why don't you join us?"

"I feel like I'm monopolizing your time with Andy. I'll have to pass tonight."

Beth slowed down behind a buggy. "You're family. Were you surprised when Mom invited you over for Sunday dinner?"

"That was sweet of her. And she said Missi will be there. It'll be good to see your old shadow."

After passing the buggy in a clear patch of road, her friend sped up. "I can't believe how late it is. I need to get back to meet the plumber."

They reached the B&B moments later. Beth parked the SUV in her normal spot. Except for Selena's rental, there were no other vehicles there. The two hugged before going their separate ways.

Selena quickly changed into a dress. She was looking forward to going out to dinner with her grandmother. Noise from the hallway drew her attention.

"Again, I apologize about being late. We're short this week and I'm filling in. The last job took longer than planned." Beth must be leading the plumber to one of the rooms. *That man's voice seems so familiar.*

The cheery sound of her friend's words resounded right outside her door. "Let's start in the room at the end of the hallway, then you can work right down the line."

"Sounds like a good plan."

Where have I heard that man's speech before? The creaking noise of a door being opened slipped in from outside her room.

Beth's voice was softer, as if it was muffled. "No offense, but since we've got guests, I'll be staying in the room while you work."

"No problem."

Though her curiosity was nagging, Selena left her suite and moved in the direction of the parking lot. *It's as if I know that man, but from where?*

Her feet came to a complete stop yards away from her rental. A white work van now sat in the lot, cargo door hanging open. Selena's gaze drifted to the emblem and name plastered on the passenger door.

"This can't be happening." With surety, Selena knew she'd identified the owner of the voice she'd overheard inside the B&B. The same man whose name was plastered on the utility vehicle. A man she hadn't seen in ten years... *Trey Brubaker.*

Chapter Three

Trey took a deep breath before proceeding. "There was a military uniform hanging up in the bathroom. The name on the jacket was Harper. I think it belonged to Selena."

"There's got to be more than one Harper in the service. Are you sure this was her?" Reed's voice was full of shock.

"No. But I got the distinct feeling it was. Do you remember Selena's friend, Beth Rutledge?"

"Wasn't she a couple years behind us? Cute girl with a pretty smile, if I remember."

"Yep, that's the one. She manages the B&B in Paradise."

"Hmm, is she still as attractive as she used to be?"

Trey pulled into the grocery store lot. He wanted to pick up a bouquet of flowers for his date with Rose. The morning clouds had parted and the sweet scent of freshly mowed hay from a nearby field filled his lungs.

"Isn't that just like you, thinking about girls? Well, you're too late. She's married and her last name is Warren. And by the way, Beth is not as adorable as she once was... she's even prettier. And very kind. She sent along a small plate of cookies—which I claimed."

"Why am I not surprised?" Reed laughed. "Did Beth recognize you?"

"She did. Told me I haven't changed one bit."

"Then I doubt Selena was staying there. I mean, if that were my friend you had dumped years ago, I'd still hold a grudge."

Trey finally reached the case where the flowers were displayed. "Maybe. Who knows? It's beyond my paygrade."

His friend's voice was quieter now. "If it was Selena, what would you do?"

Ah, the million-dollar question... "I would, I would... never mind. It doesn't matter. I'm sure Selena Harper forgot about me years ago. She's probably married to some great guy, has two kids and lives in a house with a white picket fence."

"And you wish it was you."

"Stop it. I wonder what Rose's favorite color is?"

"Pink, why?"

Trey held the phone at arm's length and stared at it briefly before returning it to his ear. "Wow, that was quick. What, are you the official historian on Rose Sheppard?"

"N-no. We're just c-close f-f-friends."

A chill trickled down Trey's spine. "Wait. Do you and Rose have something going on? If so, tell me now. I don't want to step on your toes."

"Rose is sweet, but she's never been interested in me. That girl has always been intrigued with you and no one else. Today's a special day for her and I hope it goes well. I just can't believe it took you so long to ask her out."

A lot was running through Trey's mind. "Pink, you say?"

"Yep. By the way, you cost me ten bucks."

"Say again?"

"The guys and I had a bet about when you'd finally ask Rose out. I lost, because I thought it would be last year."

"What? You had a pool on when Rose and I would go out? What, does everyone know about the date?"

"It's a small office, buddy. And everyone can tell Rose is infatuated with you... has been since you hired her." Reed's voice changed. "Glad you finally noticed that lady. She's really special. You better treat her right or I'll kick your butt. Hanging up now. The game's about to start."

"Yeah. Thanks. Bye."

Trey grabbed a bouquet of fresh cut flowers from the refrigerated case. The bunch of roses he selected were pink. *How would Reed know Rose's favorite color?* There had also been something in Reed's tone just before he'd hung up, but Trey couldn't identify it. And why did his friend end the call so abruptly?

A swift movement of a woman dressed in military camo captured his attention as she walked by. Trey's mouth dried up. The female soldier was about the same height as Selena and her hair was brown... like his girl's had been. *Wait. Could it be her?* Maybe Selena wasn't even a soldier anymore. But suppose she was and this was her?

Trey followed the lady into the checkout line, one customer between them. *If it is her, what should I say?* Trey's mind raced, trying to come up with a good line, but what do you say to a girl you loved a thousand years ago, when you were young? One that he'd dumped… for her sake. At least that was his story.

The customer in front of him addressed the lady. "Excuse me, ma'am. Are you in the service?"

The soldier slowly turned to face the man. "Yes, sir. Army Corps of Engineers."

"I'd like to thank you for your service."

The two shook hands. "And thank you for your support." Trey's pulse returned from triple digits. The nameplate on the uniform read "Smith."

***

The sun was directly overhead when Trey parked his SUV along the curb at the address Rose had provided. The house sat along a side street in Leola and, by the design, appeared to have been built in the '60s. Despite the age, the exterior was immaculately maintained. As soon as Trey opened the car door, the competing fragrances of daylilies and roses greeted him. All along the white picket fence and the foundation of the house, beautiful rows of blooms abounded.

He was halfway to the door when she appeared. He'd always thought Rose was pretty, but the beauty of the woman standing before him this morning took his breath away. Her blue eyes were shining, beckoning him to come closer. That long blonde hair cascaded to her shoulders. But the thing that swept him off his feet was Rose's smile.

"Hey, mister. You're right on time."

"Hi, Rose." He offered her the bouquet, suddenly thinking how meager this bunch was compared to the foliage in the yard. "This is the first time I've seen you in a dress. You look gorgeous today."

Her smile deepened, accompanied by a tinge of pink on her cheeks. Rose accepted the flowers and pressed them to her face. "Thank you. Roses are my favorite and these are lovely. Excuse me for a second while I put these in water. When I come back, I'll introduce you to my family. They're out working in the garden."

"Okay. I'll be right here, waiting."

Within seconds, Rose returned and placed one hand to the side of her mouth, as if she were sharing a secret. "Thank you for saving me. Saturdays are always work days in the garden."

After sending a wink his way, she took Trey's hand and led him into the backyard. While the house's frontage was small, the backyard was enormous. The soil had been worked and the result was a tidy truck patch. Luscious green rows of tomatoes, corn, peas and beans stood proudly under the sun with nary a weed in sight.

Rose cupped her hand to her mouth and called out, "Trey's here. Would everyone like to say hello?"

From the greenery, three people emerged. The man was short, but carried himself with an air of self-assuredness. Rose's mother (the resemblance was uncanny) offered a welcoming smile. But when the third person stepped forward, Trey had to do a double-take. The woman standing before him looked so much like Rose that Trey had to glance to his left to make sure his date was still there.

The father's greeting was brusque, yet the mother's reaction was full of grace and kindness. Rose then directed his attention to the other girl. "Trey, I'd like to introduce you to my twin sister, Lily."

A smile slowly covered the other girl's face. "It's good to finally meet you. I've heard so much about you over the last two years, I feel as if I know you."

A sinking feeling began to crawl through his mind. Trey knew literally nothing about Rose or her family, yet she had told her kin about him. "It's a pleasure to meet all of you. This is quite a garden you have here. And the flowers out front, exquisite. It's plain to see you take great pride in them."

The mother's face shined at the compliment. "Thank you, but the two blooms we take greatest delight in are our daughters, Rose and Lily. Maybe we could sit a spell and get to know you. Would you like a glass of tea?"

"That sounds like a winner."

Rose led him to the gazebo. Overflowing baskets of flowers were perched on the railing. Not only the sight, but the fragrance brought up images of a fairy garden. An overhead fan made the oasis cool, despite the heat of the sun. Within minutes, Mrs. Sheppard returned and they were all seated around the iron table—Rose to his right and Lily to his left. The twin he'd just met didn't say much, but her stare was unnerving.

Mr. Sheppard watched Trey suspiciously, like a nesting swallow watches a crow flying nearby. "Rose told us a lot about you. I'd like to hear your version."

Trey stuttered and stammered for the next twenty minutes under a barrage of questions. Without warning, the older man drained his glass and stood. "Well, we're burning daylight. Been nice to meet you, but those weeds won't pull themselves. You two run along and make sure you have my daughter back by nine." With that, he turned and headed to the garden.

Rose's mother waited until he was out of earshot before whispering, "Ignore George. You're not teenagers anymore. Enjoy yourselves and have fun."

Lily lingered after both parents departed. She offered her hand to Trey and smiled. "I'm envious. Are you sure the two of you don't need some company? I could get changed and be ready... really quick."

He wasn't certain, but Trey detected some tension between the women. *Sibling rivalry?* Rose smiled. "Not this time, but maybe later."

"Okay. Text me if you get bored. Bye." Lily again offered her hand as a farewell and squeezed Trey's very tightly.

Rose led Trey through the house, where she retrieved her purse and a light wrap. She was quiet until they were in the vehicle and he had pulled into traffic.

Rose suddenly giggled. "You took that well."
"What do you mean?"
"The interrogation."

He pondered her choice of words. "I can imagine that I would act a little like your dad if someone came to date my little girl."

"Really?" There was surprise in her tone.

Taking his eyes off the road, he glanced at her. "I think so. That's how men are, you know?"

Again, her face colored. "I meant the date part. Is this really truly a date, or am I just dreaming?"

"No, you're not dreaming, Rose."

"Wow. So, this is what it feels like?"

It was his turn to chuckle. "Don't tell me you've never been on a date before." Rose shook her head. "Not even high school?"

"Nope."

"I find that hard to believe. As pretty as you are, I'm certain you had to beat the boys back with a stick."

"This may seem old-fashioned, but both Lily and I followed my dad's advice. Well, at least I did."

"Which was?"

"Don't waste your time on boys. Save yourself and wait for the right man to come along."

Trey could feel his face heat. "Well, then. I don't know what to say."

The ride was suddenly silent. "Trey, may I make a confession?"

"Uh, sure."

The warm touch of her hand on his arm felt wonderful. "Y-you're the first man I ever brought home. This really is my first date... and, so you know... I'm glad it was you."

Chapter Four

Selena aimed the rental out of the senior facility's lot, heading for the state highway. Her grandmother Esther sat in the passenger seat. Because of the concentrated scent of her grandmother's gardenia perfume, Selena had rolled the windows down.

"This is nice. A girl's day out. Your mother and I used to do this a couple of times a month. I'd drive down south to visit and, even though you were little, we used to take you along. Do you remember any of that?"

Selena flashed back to that time. It became a little hard to breathe. "I don't remember that much about Mom. She was so young when she died."

Esther was looking out the passenger window. "It was hard, losing my baby. I don't even understand how I got through it all. I was just so thankful we had you. You were the spitting image of my little girl. And look at you now. You followed her footsteps and joined the nursing corps. And to think you were promoted to captain."

"That was an unfortunate blessing."

"I don't understand."

"Less than a week after my promotion, the Army announced they're cutting back the nursing corps. Since I was one of the least senior in my rank, my position was the first to be chopped."

Esther touched her arm. "What does that mean? Are you being downgraded or kicked out?"

"I'm going to the reserves. My plan was to do thirty in the service. I can still get that, but not as a full-time soldier."

Her grandmother fell silent for a few miles. "I see. And this furlough is your opportunity to determine where you want to live, where you want to set down roots?"

"Exactly. Dad moved us around quite a bit, but I wanted to look at Lancaster first. I had lots of good memories here, but the biggest reason is because you're here." The next words came out clearly, but exacted a cost. "You are the only connection I have to my past. I really hope I can find something close to you."

From the corner of her eye, Selena caught the quick wipe of tissue across her grandmother's cheek. "No matter where you lived, you kept in contact. I have no reason to doubt we'll always be close. I appreciate the sentiment, but live your life. Find what makes you happy and follow your heart."

Selena remembered the story well. Esther had grown up in rural east Tennessee. Then one day, a man knocked on her parents' door. His car had broken down and he needed to use the phone. But after his vehicle had been repaired, he came back to visit her—time and again. A year later, they tied the knot and moved with his job to Vermont. Over sixty years ago.

"Can you tell me about my mom? Did she lead a happy life?"

For the rest of the ride, Esther filled Selena's ears with stories, most of which Selena knew, but not all. The takeaway for Selena was that, though her mom's life was short, she had lived it to the fullest. Joint emotions of pride and sorrow filled her when Esther told her that Selena was hands down the greatest blessing in her mother's life.

They ate at a waterfront restaurant before taking in the art festival. This really wasn't her thing, but Esther seemed to enjoy it. Selena's thoughts were concentrated on her mom, more so than they had been for years. Esther didn't notice, chatting along as they sat on a bench on the boardwalk. Before them, the mighty Susquehanna flowed into the Chesapeake. In the sky above, bald eagles and osprey floated in the sun. The distant clouds to the east were slowly growing darker, with tinges of orange adding color to their glory. Evening shadows were getting long.

Esther pointed at a low cloud in the distance. "When you were a little girl, we would watch the clouds and talk about the shapes they made. Do you remember?"

"I do."

After taking a deep breath, her grandmother continued. "It's funny how your perspective changes. Now when I see clouds, all I can think of is the glory of God. That He designs everything. I don't understand how, with the complexity of the universe, but I believe God knows the number of hairs on every head." Esther squeezed Selena's hand. "In my heart, I know He has something special planned for you. I can feel it. Can you?"

"I wish I did, Grandma. I wish I did."

***

"I'm really impressed with the flowers at your home. Did you plant any of them?"

Rose couldn't help but smile. "Some. I love gardening. You could say it's my escape from reality. Do you have a garden?"

Trey shook his head. "No. My life is work. Now that I've seen your place, I wish I had an outlet like you do. I think I could get into having a beautiful backyard like yours. Pretty sure I've never seen any place as lovely."

"Really? You truly like flowers and aren't just joking with me?"

"Absolutely."

The idea suddenly appeared in her mind. "Can we call an audible?"

"A what?"

"An audible... like what a quarterback does when he doesn't like the way the defense is lined up."

"I didn't know you liked football."

Rose felt her lips curl at the look of wonder in his eyes. "I have cousins that live in Peabody, Massachusetts. My uncle took me and Lily to a Patriots playoff game when we were younger. It snowed like crazy. But the atmosphere of being at Gillette Stadium, the roar of the crowd and the exhilaration of Tom Brady leading the Pats to a comeback from behind in an overtime win... ah, a cherished memory."

Trey's expression changed. Rose had worked, and watched him, long enough to know he was about to tease her. "Oh, I didn't realize you were a Patriots fan. I root for the Ravens. Maybe I should pull over and let you out."

Rose couldn't help but laugh. "Don't be a hater. Now, back to the subject. Since you like gardens so much, may I suggest we detour for a couple of hours? That is, unless you have your heart set on the art festival."

"Uh, no. A change would be fine. You're the one who suggested going to the festival."

"I'm not really an art fan. I only wanted to spend time with you. To be honest, I didn't think you'd want to go... out with me, I mean."

After a long hesitation, Trey responded. "I'm beginning to be sorry I didn't ask sooner. Now, where shall we go?"

Rose took a deep breath and Trey felt the lady was about to share something earthshaking. "I want to take you to my happy place. Somewhere I go a couple of times a month. I often bring a book and sit there, dreaming about the future." She reached across the seat and touched his arm. "You're the first person I've ever wanted to share this with."

His SUV rolled to a stop. They were sitting at a stoplight on the New Holland Pike in Eden. Trey's blue eyes were bright shining beacons, even in daylight. "Where do you want to take me?"

"Longwood Gardens. The flowers are stunning."

"Somehow, I doubt they could ever compare to your beauty."

The day turned out to be the best of Rose's life. Longwood had a special sparkle. After sharing the afternoon, the pair decided to drive down to Havre de Grace for dinner and a walk along the water. Being with Trey was so natural. The mealtime had been pleasant. Trey opened up about his life. How he had to become the breadwinner at eighteen when his dad walked out. That he and his girlfriend had plans to attend college together, but he'd broken it off for her sake.

Side by side, they walked along the boardwalk. "Do you keep in touch with her?"

"No, I haven't seen her since high school."

"I'm sorry it didn't work out."

Trey sighed. "God has a plan for our lives. He led me down a different path than I wanted at the time, that's all."

"I hope you find happiness."

He stopped and turned Rose to face him. "I'm beginning to think I could be on the right road, now. I'm sorry I never realized how wonderful you are."

It was hard to catch her breath. Trey's lips were so close. Could it be the moment she dreamed about was going to happen?

He released her hands and touched her face.

"Th-thank you. You're pretty amazing yourself."

He rubbed his nose against hers. This was it! She could sense his lips were about to touch hers. Pleasant tingles climbed up her limbs, converging on her heart. Suddenly, an old woman's voice split the evening air.

"Trey? Trey Brubaker? Is that you?"

***

Despite not hearing it for years, Trey immediately knew the speaker. He released Rose and pivoted. Sitting on a bench was an old lady. "Esther?"

The woman's face split in a wide smile. "We were just talking about you."

We? He became aware of the woman sitting next to the elderly lady. The deep tan on her face couldn't hide those eyes. She'd changed. The hair was shorter and her face thinner. But those eyes... he'd recognize them anywhere. "Selena?"

The woman stood and offered her hand. It was trembling, just like he realized his were, when he took it. "Good to see you again, Trey. It's been a while." Selena turned to face Rose. "I'm Selena Harper. Trey and I knew each other in high school."

From the corner of his eye, Trey noticed how blanched Rose's face had become. Still, his date shook his ex-girlfriend's hand. "I'm Rose Sheppard. Trey told me a little bit about you."

Selena swallowed hard. "Good stuff, I hope."

"He spoke of you with reverence and respect."

Selena returned her attention to Trey. "I didn't mean to interrupt your date. Sorry about that. Nice to see you again."

"That's okay, but I need to ask you something. Did you ever achieve your dream of becoming an Army nurse?"

Those eyes now bored into his soul, making him feel naked. "I did. I was recently promoted to captain. What about you?"

Before he could reply, Rose interrupted. "What's it like being a nurse in the armed forces? Do you get to travel to exotic places?"

"A few. I've enjoyed the ride. I'm stationed on Oahu right now."

"Hawaii? Wow. I've never been to that state, but want to visit it badly. Is it as pretty as they make it look on television?"

"TV doesn't do an adequate job. The green of the plants contrasts with the blue of the ocean, making it look like a dream."

"And the flowers... I can only imagine they're everywhere. Is it really paradise?"

"It is. It never gets very cold or too hot. We get a lot of rain so that keeps everything green and lush. The trade winds bring a gentle breeze, carrying the scent of plumeria with it."

"Plumeria? Even the name sounds like heaven. It doesn't grow here, but they have it at Longwood in the conservatory."

The conversation between the two women continued for several minutes, as if they were the oldest of friends. Trey wasn't sure what he'd expected to happen if and when he ever met Selena Harper again, but it surely wasn't this.

"I just had a thought," Rose said. "My sister and I run the youth fellowship at our church. We've been talking about careers lately. Would you mind joining us sometime and talking to the kids about your experiences?"

"I'm only in the area for a short while."

The sky was starting to darken as the sun set behind Selena and her grandmother. "I'm sorry. I wouldn't want to monopolize your time."

Selena studied Rose briefly. "It wouldn't be an imposition, but we'd need to do it in the next week or two."

"That would be wonderful."

Trey stared in disbelief as the pair shared cell numbers.

Selena glanced at Esther. "Grandma, it's getting late. Shall we head home?"

"Whenever you're ready."

Selena directed her attention back to the couple. "It was a pleasure to meet you, Rose." Her eyes again touched his. "Nice to see you again, Trey."

And just like that, the girl he'd once loved and thought about daily walked off into the darkening night... acting as if he'd never existed.

Chapter Five

Beth slid into the chair next to Selena. The weather had changed and the morning's light drizzle left a glaze on the grass and the flowers. Her friend had prepared fried potatoes, sausage and eggs for breakfast.

"Good morning. How was your weekend?"

"Uh... eventful, to say the least. How was yours? You and Anderson went to Ohio, right?"

There was a funny gleam in Beth's eye. After wiping her lips, Selena's friend replied, "We drove out to see his grandparents. They raised Anderson and are so sweet to us. They'll always hold a special place in my heart."

At least you have a family. "Then I'm glad you took the weekend off. The vouchers for breakfast at the tea room were okay, but you're a better chef. Besides, I could have used your friendship this weekend."

"What happened?"

"I told you I was planning on taking my grandma out to dinner on Saturday." Beth nodded. "She wanted to go to an arts festival in Maryland. The village was right along the bay."

"Did you have a good time?"

"She did. After we ate, the two of us were sitting along the water when this couple appeared. Never guess who it was."

Beth spoke and then shoved a forkful of potatoes in her mouth. "I dunno. Who?"

"Trey Brubaker... with this blonde bombshell on his arm. Grandma interrupted them just as they were about to kiss."

Her friend almost choked on the food. "What did he say when he saw it was you?"

"He wouldn't have noticed me if Grandma hadn't spoken to him."

Beth's complexion paled. "How did he react?"

"He didn't get a chance to say a whole lot, but his girlfriend did."

"Oh, no. Was it a bad confrontation?"

Selena paused. "Actually, just the opposite. Rose appears to be a nice lady. It actually felt like we were old and close friends. She was impressed I was a nurse in the armed services."

"Well, I'm glad of that, but what about Trey?"

"After I got over the shock of seeing him, I kept watching him out of the corner of my eye."

"And?"

"I'm not sure, but I think he was frightened, and I don't know why. Perhaps it was the shock of seeing me again or maybe because I was speaking with Rose. Maybe Trey thought I'd fill her mind with stories of all the horrible things he did."

Beth touched her hand. "What evil things?"

"There weren't any. Trey was always the perfect gentleman. Down inside, I knew he was trying to take care of his family. I really believe he broke up with me because he thought it would be best for me, not him." Sighing, Selena looked out across the glistening fields. "I thought one day he'd reach out. That he'd tell me that he'd waited for me all these years and I was his one true love in life. Guess I was the fool, lingering in the shadows all this time. Sowing my wishes... in vain."

"I'm sorry. I should have told you about it, but I didn't have a chance before Andy and I headed to Ohio. Remember when I told you we were doing bathroom upgrades last week?"

Selena turned her gaze to Beth. "The plumber was Trey, wasn't it? I saw his van parked outside when I left. Did he recognize you?"

"Not at first. But I did ask him about his life... you know... to satisfy your curiosity. Here's what I got. He's not married, but still supports his mother. Trey put his sisters through college, but never went himself. Life was kind to him and he fell into a couple of good business deals. The end result is he built his plumbing business into quite a success."

"That's nice. Did he ask about me?"

Beth shook her head. "He hinted about you a couple of times, but I didn't know how you would want me to answer, so I avoided the subject altogether." The pair shared a long look. "Isn't it odd, how he happened to be the plumber Ellie Campbell picked and then you run into him at some random town along the Chesapeake? You know, there are no coincidences in life, but I wonder why God arranged these circumstances?" Beth's cheeks reddened. "I'm sorry if you feel like I'm sticking my nose in your business."

Selena shook her head. "Oh, don't worry about that. I'll let you make it up to me."

"How?"

"You see, Trey's girlfriend told me she and her sister run a youth group at their church. Rose wants me to talk to the kids about my career."

"What? Wait. Do I have this right? His girlfriend wants *you* to speak at *her* church group?"

"Um-hmm."

"Are you going to do it?"

"Actually, we *both* are."

"Both? Did I hear you correctly?"

"Yep, as in you and I."

Beth pushed back her chair. "How did I get pulled into this?"

"You're my friend, aren't you?"

"Of course."

"Well, you and I are meeting Rose and her sister for lunch tomorrow."

"But why would you have me come along?"

"Three reasons. First, I want the sides to be even. She's bringing her sister, so I'm taking mine. Second, I was hoping you could help me dig a little deeper into the whole Rose-Trey relationship thing. It would sound weird if I asked the questions you're going to ask."

"*I'm* going to ask? What exactly does that mean?"

"Come on, Beth. We're going to be playing good cop, bad cop, but we'll plan your lines ahead of time."

"Oh, I see. Now you're being devious."

"Nope, you're the one who's going to play that role."

"Why would I do that?"

"For the third reason."

Beth wrinkled her nose as she stared at Selena. "Which is?"

"I want to see if this Rose woman is really as sweet as she appears. Nobody I know is as perfect as that girl seems to be."

***

"Well, well. I expected a bigger smile on your face this morning." Trey couldn't quite decide if Reed was teasing or being serious. "How'd the date go?"

"Oh, the initial part was fine. Rose took me to Longwood."

Reed's face turned slightly pink. "Unbelievable. That's her favorite place in the world... and she took you there. On your first date? How lucky is that?"

Once again, Trey pondered how Reed knew so much about Rose. "She sure did. Afterwards, we drove down to Havre de Grace for dinner."

His friend directed his focus on the computer screen in front of him. "I bet she ordered broiled crabcakes."

"Actually, we both did."

The swiftness with which Reed pivoted to face him surprised Trey. "Another of Rose's faves. Then what?"

"Well, that's where it got strange." Trey noted that Reed's lips had turned into a fine white line, but the man didn't say anything. "We were walking and this lady called my name. It turned out to be Selena's grandmother."

"Selena? As in Selena Harper?"

"Yep, that's the one."

"Not what I expected. Did she give you an update on her granddaughter?"

"She didn't have to. Selena was there, too."

Reed walked around the counter so they were side by side. His voice was low and soft. "What did she say? Did she still look the same? Is she married?"

"Selena said hello to me. Then, when I introduced her to Rose, I believe I could have jumped in the bay and it wouldn't have mattered... to either of them."

"I don't understand."

"Rose appeared to be quite impressed with Selena's choice of a career. My ex-girlfriend is an Army nurse."

Reed touched his arm. "Did they talk about you?"

"At that moment in time, I'm not sure either one of them remembered I existed."

His friend's face paled. "Oh, my. You don't think that Selena..."

Trey felt like punching Reed. "No, they both acted like they were long-lost friends. All that talk about Hawaii and flowers and Germany and tropical winds and coconuts and I don't know what else. I almost died when Rose asked Selena to speak at her church." Reed was eyeing him strangely. "Something about talking to the youth group."

"Rose and Lily run youth fellowship together. This year, they've had a number of people come in to talk about their careers."

Once again, an eerie feeling walked across Trey's shoulders. "You seem to know an awful lot about Rose. Are you sure there's not something going on between you two?"

His friend's face turned pink. "Like I've told you before, Rose Sheppard is not interested in me. She likes you."

Before they could continue, the door separating the shop from the business office swung open. Rose sauntered through. She wore her normal blue jeans along with a tropical flowered top. Above Rose's right ear, she sported a small flower. "Happy Monday." She slid a paper plate full of fruit tarts onto the counter.

Reed beat Trey to the compliment. "They smell heavenly. What kind are they?"

Her smile grew. "Strawberry-rhubarb. Lily and I made these yesterday for the youth fellowship. I figured you guys might like some." Rose's eyes drifted to meet Trey's. Hers were sparkling. "Morning, stranger. How was your weekend?"

It was as if this lady were a lighthouse, offering hope and shelter in a storm. All of the worry within him vanished. "Saturday was great, but Sunday was kind of lonely."

"Hmm. We might have to work on that."

"You look very beautiful today. What's with the flower in your hair?"

"It was fun meeting Selena. I think she's the first person I've ever met that lived in Hawaii." Rose's smile grew. "I spent some time yesterday surfing the web about Hawaii and Hawaiian culture. Did you know that when a woman wears a flower above her right ear, it means she's unattached?"

"No, I didn't. And if a lady wears it above her left ear?"

Rose didn't answer right away. There was a glint in her eyes. "Then she's in a relationship."

The room fell into total silence. While all of Trey's attention was focused on Rose, he considered how much prettier she would look with that flower on the other side of her head. The silent encounter continued until Trey realized they were the center of attention. He could feel eyes watching them—not only Reed's, but everyone else in the shop.

Rose must have sensed it as well. A slight blush started in her neck and worked upwards. "Well, I need to get moving. Those invoices won't post themselves. Oh, by the way, I'd like to take a half-day tomorrow."

"Uh, sure. Are you doing anything special?"

"Kind of. Lily and I are meeting Selena for tea and sandwiches. We want to talk to her about this coming Sunday. I don't want our friend to feel rushed."

"What's this Sunday?"

"Like every other week, it's the day after Saturday, silly." She giggled, but several of the guys joined in with raucous laughter.

The frivolity stopped when Trey whipped around and stared down his employees.

Rose's smile quickly faded and her words were suddenly whisper quiet. "We're inviting her to youth fellowship to talk about her career. You could come if you want."

"I, uh, don't know..." Reed quickly elbowed Trey in the ribs. "We'll see."

"Okay. Guess I'll be going."

"Wait. Are you busy tonight?"

Her eyes widened. "I was planning on driving down to the gardens. Why do you ask?"

"Want to have supper with me?"

Her whole face shined. "I'd love that, but how about we eat there, too? There's special music going on tonight—Kathy Mattea is being featured."

"That sounds great. I'll pick you up at five?"

Rose nodded and then leaned in closer. "Can I ask why?"

"I want to see more of you, if that's okay."

Taking a quick breath, she briefly touched his arm. "I'd love it. Gotta get moving now." She held her hand to the side of her mouth as if to share a secret. "The boss here is a slave driver, you know?" And with that, she swished through the door and back into the office.

Trey knew all eyes were focused on him, but right now, it didn't matter. He turned to Reed and kept his voice low. "You and I are doing lunch tomorrow."

His friend smacked him on the shoulder. "Score! Where ya taking me?"

"Sophie Miller's tea room."

Reed's smile vanished. "Why there?"

"I believe you know."

"Enlighten me."

"Because that's where Rose is meeting Selena. I will not allow a mistake I made when I was a kid to ruin my future as an adult."

Chapter Six

"I want to go on record right now that I'm doing this under protest," Beth decreed defiantly.

Selena rolled her eyes. "Duly noted. Regardless of your objection, we'll implement the plan just as we discussed to achieve our objectives. Let's roll."

The pair stepped out of Selena's rental car and scurried across the parking lot. The scent of the flowers that lined the walkway and covered the arch normally would have created a romantic and dreamy atmosphere, but not today. Beth wasn't looking forward to the encounter with the Sheppard twins.

When she and Selena had discussed the strategy for the lunch meeting, it was plain to see Selena had given it a lot of thought. And one thing became readily apparent to Beth. Though her friend didn't admit it, Selena was still very much intrigued with Trey Brubaker... and his relationship with this Rose Sheppard woman.

The bell on the door tinkled when Selena opened it. There at the podium stood Sophie Miller, a smile gracing her beautiful face. "Morning, Beth. Who's your friend?"

"This is Selena Harper. She was my best friend in high school."

The trio chatted for a few moments. The Sheppard girls had not yet arrived.

While Beth socialized, Selena perused the collection of photographs hanging on the wall. She paused at one in particular. "Beth, what's this picture? Everyone in the photo is bald. Wait, is that you... and your mom... and your stepdad? Hey, I know the background building. It's the bed and breakfast where I'm staying."

Beth stood behind her. "Good eye. That was taken about four years ago. And yes, that's my family, among many others."

Selena's face turned ashen. "Everyone shaved their heads to support someone going through chemo, didn't they?"

"Yes. Ellie Campbell. I told you the B&B I manage used to be her home. The situation looked bleak for her, so she moved 'back home', as she called it. Ellie confided in me that if things didn't turn out well, she didn't want her children to remember their new home with sorrow. Her husband, Henry, stayed by her side night and day for months. More than once, I heard him tell Ellie they had vowed to love each other forever, in sickness or in health. He'd always hold Ellie and tell her he intended to do exactly that, until his dying day. It was a difficult period for Ellie and, well, for many of us. Lots of prayers made it to Heaven on her behalf.

That kind woman has touched so many people's lives."

Selena faced her friend. "I'm sorry."

Beth didn't answer, but instead gently ran her finger over Ellie's image in the print. "That photo was taken the day she came back from the hospital after the first round of chemo. Over thirty of us were there to cheer her on."

Selena touched her friend's hand. "But Ellie survived, didn't she?"

Beth wiped a hand across her cheeks. "Of course. Ellie's the strongest and most determined woman I've ever met. After chemo failed, she had a bone marrow transplant. Her brother Kevin was the donor. It was a long recovery for her." Beth pointed at another framed print on the wall. "And this one was taken the day of the party when Ellie returned back home, to the house she and Henry share with their children. Many tears were shed that day, but they were of happiness and thanksgiving. Our prayers had been answered."

The bell again sounded. Two beautiful blonde ladies entered. The one with a rosebud in her hair over her right ear stepped forward and called, "Hey, Selena. Thanks for meeting with us today. I'd like you to meet my sister, Lily."

Selena said hello and introduced Beth. Sophie returned with a stack of menus. "Any preferences where you'd like to sit?"

Beth was going to suggest the outside garden her friend Josh Miller had created, but Rose beat her to the punch. "The roses are in bloom. Can you seat us in the outside patio?"

As Sophie led the way, Beth smiled inside. *Hmm. Rose wears a rosebud and sits amongst the roses? How funny, like a riddle from a Doctor Seuss book.* Beth made a mental note to share this with Selena later.

After ordering their tea, Rose spoke at length about the youth program at church. "I think that kids these days are in a rough spot. With all the garbage on the web and pressure of social media, they need exposure to all the good influences they can get. That's why Lily and I decided to introduce them to people who are positive role models, such as yourself. People that exhibit compassion, courage and excellent morals in their journey."

Selena swished the tea in her cup before taking another sip. "Why select me? Because I'm a nurse?"

Beth couldn't help but notice how Rose set down her cup and focused all of her attention on Selena. "Mostly. Forgive me for saying it because this may sound strange, but I felt a strong connection with you when we met in Havre de Grace. As if God had brought us together for a purpose."

Selena and Beth exchanged a glance before Selena responded. "What do you think is the reason?"

Rose shrugged. "I'm not sure, but I'm certain He has a purpose."

Lily spoke for the first time. "You have to forgive my sister. She is dogmatic in her belief that everything happens for a reason. As a result, Rose looks for the silver lining in every situation."

Beth entered the conversation. "And you don't feel that way?"

"No. I believe God has milestones picked out for us and at those markers, we have decisions to make. The choices we make affect how our lives will play out." Lily's eyes roved around the table. "In my opinion, our lives are a matter of free will, not pre-destination."

Beth tilted her head to take in Lily. "In other words, you see certain things, such as Rose and Selena meeting along the Chesapeake, as pure coincidence?"

"Yep. Just a random roll of the die. Don't you agree?"

Something about the younger woman irked Beth. "Not really. I believe God is in total control. He created us and guides our lives. It's entirely probable He intended for them to meet."

Lily smirked. "In other words, you believe we're just automatons who have no control over our destiny. That's bizarre. One needs to be in charge of the hand we're dealt. Why would God create a bunch of humans He fully controls? He has angels, which are much more wonderful than mere mortals. Instead, I believe God wants us to freely make the decision to worship Him."

Rose shook her head. "Lily, please. These are my friends. I don't want you to offend them, okay?"

Lily shifted her head to face her sister. "I wasn't trying to do that. You called them your friends. I hope in time they'll be mine as well. In my opinion, friends should be able to speak openly. Would you rather I leave?"

Beth and Selena shared a confused look. The obvious undercurrents in the relationship were about to boil over.

But when Rose reached for and squeezed her sister's hand, the conflict seemed to fizzle. "Of course not. You and me, we're sisters and best friends, forever." Rose returned her attention to Beth. "What do you do?"

"I'm the innkeeper at the Paradise Bed and Breakfast."

"Do you like your position?"

"Actually, I see it not just as a job, but as a ministry. I'm here not only to take care of the guests by feeding them breakfast and keeping their rooms clean, but I try to set an example of hospitality. Jesus was always welcoming to everyone, so that's how I try to be."

Rose laughed. "I get it. 'Be not forgetful to entertain strangers, for thereby some have entertained angels unaware'. That's one of my favorite passages from Hebrews. Maybe you would like to talk to our youth as well?"

"I would be honored." Out of sight of the twins, Selena nudged Beth's leg with her foot. Without even trying, they'd accomplished their first objective. Now, to dig into Trey and Rose's relationship... "I've never been to Havre de Grace. What's it like?"

Rose smiled, but studied her teacup before responding. "It was the first time I'd ever been there. Trey and I were going to spend the day at the arts festival in town, but we did an audible instead. We only had dinner there."

Selena looked puzzled. "You listened to an audio book?"

The girl sporting the flower in her hair giggled. "No, it's a football reference. Let me come clean—I'm a Patriots fan."

"That's a brave thing to say, seeing as you are living in Eagle, Steeler and Raven territory," Beth teased. "Have you and Trey ever been to an NFL game to see them play?"

Rose's face turned bright red. "No. Saturday was our first date."

Selena was astounded. "But the two of you looked so comfortable together, as if you'd known each other for a while."

"I told you we make our own opportunities," Lily jumped in. "And they have known each other for a long time. Perhaps you weren't aware that Rose works for Trey?"

Rose's head snapped to her sister. "Lily..."

"Trey came to our house two years ago to fix a leaky pipe. My sister was entranced with him. Believed she'd just met the man God picked out for her. She decided to seize the opportunity and control her destiny. It was one of those milestones we encounter along our journey."

"Lily!"

The twin had a smirk on her face. "Rose took an entry level clerical job at his company just so she could be close to the man. To do that, she gave up a great, high paying job as a logistics manager for a manufacturing company. My parents were miffed, but Rose did it anyway. Guess she figured that one day, Trey would notice and fall in love with her.

Then, voila! He finally opened his eyes and found out how totally amazing my sister is."

The table was silent. Beth could tell Rose was upset, still the lady gracefully calmed herself before speaking. "Lily, I hope I never embarrass you in public by revealing your shortcomings, like you just did about mine."

Lily appeared shaken. "Sis, in my eyes you have no shortcomings. I'm sorry if I offended you, but every word I spoke is the truth. You took that job hoping Trey would notice you. Guess what? It worked. Your dreams are coming true. I apologize if you thought I was being snarky, but I didn't mean it in a bad way."

Rose's expression changed and she smiled at her sister. "It's okay." Following a deep breath, Rose now turned to face Selena. "How about we change the subject? Please tell us more about Hawaii. I've always dreamed of going there, but I'm not sure God has that in my plans."

Lily shook her head. "You will see Hawaii, Rose, if you want to. Someday there will be a fork in the road and you'll be able to choose that direction. I have faith that you can do or be or go anywhere you wish. Of all the people in the world who deserve good things to happen, you deserve it the most."

At that moment, the door to the interior of the restaurant opened. Since their seating, the tables in the tea room had filled up. Sophie Miller led two men to a neighboring table. Both were handsome, but one was especially so. His neatly trimmed beard and athletic figure caught Beth's eye.

When she shifted her gaze to the second man, her mouth went dry. It was Trey Brubaker.

***

"I've never been to this place, have you?"

A shiver crossed Trey's shoulders as he and Reed walked from their work vans toward the strange looking building. Trey answered. "I knew it existed. I took Selena here on our first date eons ago, but haven't been inside since."

"Do they serve actual food or is this only for tea and crumpets?"

"I researched the menu online. They have soups and sandwiches. Do you even know what a crumpet is?"

Reed snickered. "Sure do. Tastykake sells them. I'm a big fan of the butterscotch variety."

"Can you please try to act cultured? I don't want everyone to think we're backwoods hicks."

"I'll put on a good front, but I can't forget my roots or the lean years. Remember when you first started this business? We had two tired old work vans built in the early '70s. For lunch, we made tomato soup out of ketchup packets we palmed from a fast-food joint. But look at how it grew."

The two had been friends since grade school. Trey knew Reed brought up the memories of their meager beginning to cheer him up.

His friend now spoke in a false British accent. "And now look at us. Having high tea together. I'm glad we're such chummy pals, old chap. Maybe after our tea, we can play cricket or polo."

"You should be committed. With friends like you, who needs enemies?" Trey shook his head. But as he reached for the handle to the door, Reed touched his arm.

"Are you sure you want to go through with this? I mean, don't you think Rose will find it strange that you show up at the same place she's having lunch with your old girlfriend?"

"Rose never told me where they were going to meet."

"Duh. This is the only tea room in Paradise."

Reed was right. This was probably a dumb idea, but his internal voice pushed him onwards. "I don't want Selena to turn Rose against me."

"And you think she will?"

"Hopefully not, but I won't chance it." Trey swung the door open. A jumbled collage of delicious scents poured out from inside—fragrant tea, flowers, freshly baked bread, grilled steak and seafood.

A pleasant lady greeted them. "Good afternoon. I'm Jessica. Here for lunch or tea?"

The place was packed. Trey quickly surveyed, but couldn't locate either Rose or Selena. "Lunch, please."

"Is outside seating acceptable?"

"Sure."

Jessica had just grabbed two laminated menus when a short, but extremely attractive lady appeared. She had a natural English accent. "I'll seat them, Jessica. Do you mind helping serve? Carol had to leave, so we're short staffed."

The older lady smiled. "I don't mind at all. I was going to seat these two gentlemen outside. G-3 is our last open table." With that, Jessica departed.

"Hello, gents. I'm Sophie Miller. Please follow me."

Sophie led them out a side door into a lovely hardscaped area, complete with flowering bushes and plants. As soon as they stepped outside, Trey noticed the four ladies. Beth Rutledge, scratch that, Beth *Warren* sat facing them. He caught the nudge she gave to the girl on her left. When that girl turned around, Trey's face warmed. It was Selena. Within half a second, the other two occupants of the table followed suit and gazed in his direction. Rose and Lily Sheppard both smiled at them.

Reed touched his shoulder and then whispered, "I think they noticed us."

"Brilliant deduction, Sherlock."

Rose quickly stood, and walked over to take Trey's hand. Her smile put his fears at rest. "Hi, Trey. This is such a wonderful treat, you showing up. Our table is large. Would you please join us?"

"That sounds great," Reed answered for them.

"Hey, Reed. Sorry I didn't notice you." The girl with the flower in her hair now faced the hostess. "Sophie, would you mind if they joined us?"

"Not at all. I'll inform the server of your decision. Enjoy your meal."

Rose's hand was warm in Trey's as she led him to the table, rearranging the chairs so Trey could sit between her and Selena. Reed ended up sitting between Selena and Beth. After introductions were made, the server arrived and took the men's orders.

"Selena was just about to tell us about what it's like to be an Army nurse living in Hawaii," Rose announced.

Trey's old girlfriend looked even more attractive than she had on Saturday. Her deep tan and pearly white teeth contrasted, only adding to her beauty. Trey forced himself to turn his attention away from Selena and focus instead on Rose. Her long, silky hair cascaded across her shoulders. *If I had to choose?*

Trey shook his head to get rid of the thought. It struck him as odd. To his left was the girl of his past. To his right sat the lady he was hoping might be his future.

The food was delicious, but the other occupants didn't seem to notice. Everyone was hanging on Selena's words as she answered every question Rose and Lily posed. They had just finished dessert when Trey glanced at his watch, he couldn't believe what time it was. It was after two!

"I didn't realize how late it is. Reed and I need to get moving. We're overdue for our afternoon appointments."

He pushed back his chair and Rose stood as well. To his surprise, she hugged him lightly and whispered in his ear, "Thank you for stopping by this afternoon."

"I hope I didn't rain on your parade."

"There's no way you could ever do that. See you tomorrow, unless you want to stop over this evening."

"Great idea. I wouldn't be able to make dinner, but how about ice cream?"

"Sounds wonderful. See you at seven?"

"Can't wait." He quickly glanced over at Selena to gauge her reaction, but she wasn't even looking in his direction. Instead, Reed appeared to be on the receiving end of her focus.

The two men left and stood between the work vans in the parking lot. Reed had a funny look on his face. "Thanks for asking me to go along, Trey."

"No problem, though we're going to have to work late to catch up."

"How do you think it went... I mean with Selena possibly changing Rose's opinion of you?"

"I think my fears were unjustified."

"I agree. Can I ask a stupid question?"

"Sure."

"Do you really care for Rose?"

Where was Reed going with this? "I'm beginning to, very much."

"And what about Selena?"

Trey hesitated. Despite the closeness of the friendship he and Reed shared, Trey wasn't ready to discuss things he himself wasn't quite sure of. Complicating matters even further, Selena didn't seem to care about him anyway. He finally answered, "What's past is past."

Reed's face turned red and the man closed his eyes tightly before continuing. "In that case, would you mind if I asked Selena out?"

Chapter Seven

Trey was a few minutes late arriving at the shop on Monday. Stepping into the office, he found it unoccupied. At his desk, he discovered two fresh donuts. A smile grew on his face. *Rose brought these.* He hadn't seen her yesterday and was hoping the two of them could chat for a few minutes before starting the day.

From somewhere in the building, the enticing scent of Columbian coffee beckoned. The distant sound of laughter floated through the walls. Curious, he walked through the door to the shop. The area was vacant except for two people. Reed was standing at the service desk while Rose was seated in his chair.

Her face lit up when she caught a glimpse of Trey.

She is so beautiful. Why didn't I ever notice her before? "Good morning, you two. What's so funny?"

The girl reached out and quickly squeezed his hand. "Good morning. I missed you yesterday. What did you do with your Sunday?"

"I took Mom and one of my sisters out to dinner. What about you?"

"Church in the morning. I drove down to Longwood for some me-time in the afternoon, and then last night we had youth fellowship. Beth and Selena were both there to talk about their careers."

"The kids loved that pair," Reed interjected.

That was a strange comment, since Reed attended the same church as Trey. "How do you know? Were you there?"

His friend's face turned pink. "Yeah. Selena and I went for a hike in the afternoon and she invited me to tag along."

Rose shook her head. "That's a shame about what happened with Selena's Army job. But I love how positive she is in the face of uncertainty."

Trey was puzzled. *Her Army job?* "What do you mean?"

Reed set down his coffee. Trey noted the logo on the paper cup was the same as the one in Rose's hand. "The Army is downsizing the number of nurses," he said. "Because Selly just got promoted, her job is being cut."

"Selly?"

The white flash of teeth in his friend's smile contrasted against his dark beard. "Selena. She said her Army buddies all called her that."

"I see. So, did she say what's she going to do?"

"She said that's one of the reasons she came to Lancaster. She's checking out the job situation here."

Rose swiveled to face Trey. "I admire her. It takes strength and good, strong character to face trials like that. I mean, she was living her work dream and just like that, it's gone."

"Does this mean Selena has moved back here for good?"

"When we were on our hike, Selly said she's only here to check out the area. At the end of the month, she's going back to Hawaii to muster out." Reed's face was abruptly sad. "I really hope she decides to move back here."

"Hmm, maybe it was in God's plan for the two of you to meet," Rose teased.

Reed winked at her. "How would Lily put it? 'You are standing at one of life's monumental crossroads... which path will you choose?'"

Rose laughed so hard she almost fell off the chair. "Please stop. Lily can't help herself. That's what she believes."

Something about the intimate way his two friends were interacting bothered Trey. The laughter stopped when he posed the question to Rose. "Okay, so then what do you believe?"

"About what?"

"About Selena showing up here."

"I'm not sure. Why would you ask?"

"You seem to have the inside track on God's intentions. Why is she here?"

A crimson tinge crept into the girl's cheeks. "Why do you feel I would know?"

"You seem to know exactly what God is doing."

Reed stepped closer to Trey. "I don't like your tone. If my joke offended you, talk to me about it, instead of giving Rose a hard time."

Why am I acting this way? Trey shook his head and then focused his full attention on Rose. "I meant no harm. It's just you're pretty smart and definitely have a better understanding of how God is at work in the world than I do." He touched Rose's arm. "I didn't mean to offend you. Sorry."

The girl's color returned to normal. She began to snicker. "It's okay."

"Did I say something funny?"

"Absolutely not. For future reference, this is my happy laugh." She handed him the cup she'd been drinking from. "Here, you can have mine. Because I know you well enough to know this is how you react when you haven't had your morning java."

"Perhaps you're right, but I don't want yours. I'll stop somewhere and get a cup."

Her lips were caught in a smile. "I'll make you some, but in the meanwhile, drink up. I should have bought three cups this morning, not just two. You're normally here before Reed and when I ran into him, I absentmindedly gave your cup to him."

"But Rose, I'm not going to take your coffee."

She was already headed back to the office when she sent the comment over her shoulder. "Please drink it. I don't mind sharing my coffee, or anything else, with you."

He watched until the door between the office and the shop closed. Reed's voice was soft. "She's a very special lady, you know? And you're a very fortunate man."

"I'm quite aware of that."

"Be careful, Trey."

He turned to face Reed. "Of what?"

"That girl is tender and full of innocence. Don't let your anger hurt her."

Trey shifted until their noses were about to touch. "And what reason would I have to be angry?"

Reed smiled and shrugged. "I'm not exactly sure. Maybe because I took your coffee." His friend offered his own cup. "Here, you can have it back."

"And put my lips where you put yours?" Anger welled up within Trey. "Keep your hands, and lips, off of things that are mine in the future."

The happiness in the man's face was gone now. "You can't have everything, Trey. And let me tell you this. Don't be jealous when I pick up the rock you've tossed aside and make it the cornerstone of my life."

"What's that supposed to mean?"

Reed drained the contents before crumpling the paper cup. He threw it in the trash before turning away. "You're supposed to be a brilliant man. Figure it out yourself."

***

Selena took her seat on the wrap-around porch. Beth was serving other patrons. While waiting, Selena glanced at her cell. Reed's morning text made her smile. Closing her eyes, her mind wandered to the future. *Is Lancaster really my destiny?*

"There's the lady of the hour. What time did *you* get in last evening? I know it was after eleven." Beth dipped out a generous portion of casserole.

Having difficulty keeping a laugh inside, a smile graced Selena's lips. "Might you be keeping an eye on me, Mrs. Warren?"

"Nope. Had a customer arrive about that time and simply noted your car wasn't in the lot." Her friend finally sat down. "Did you say prayers yet?"

"No. May I offer them with you?"

"Of course."

The two friends bowed their heads. "Good morning, Father. On this beautiful day, we want to offer our thanks for this food and the blessings you've covered us with. Please bless my friend, Beth, not just for making the food, but for her friendship. As you know, we're both approaching crossroads in our lives. For me, deciding what to do and where to live next. For Beth and Andy, finding their place in the world. And I ask this, Lord, wherever we go and whatever we do, please let us remain close at heart. Amen."

"Amen. That was beautiful. Now, where did you two go last night?"

"We spent the nightfall in Columbia, eventually. We parked my car downtown and took his to Marietta. We strolled the River Trail and finished with a twilight picnic in Columbia. The stars were beautiful."

Beth refilled her juice glass. "You two seem to be getting close, and it's only been what... two weeks?"

Selena again felt the smile on her face. "Seems longer than a couple of days. I think it's time to introduce him to Andy."

Her friend's left eyebrow raised. "Why?"

"Because you two are my family. I know you remember Reed from school, but I'd like both of you to get to know him—and then let me know what you think. Reed is becoming important to me."

"Selena Harper. Are you and Reed getting serious?"

Her face warmed. "Not really, but it's been so long since I dated." A glance at Beth's face told Selena joking was about to commence. "Please don't tease me."

"Why? Don't take my sole joy in life away from me."

"Come on. Let's change the subject."

Beth sighed. "Against my better judgment... but one more thing. Andy and I were thinking about driving up to Caledonia Saturday morning. Why don't you and Reed join us for a hike?"

"That sounds like fun."

Her friend wiped her mouth with a napkin. "I do need to warn you. Andy found this little farmette up there that's for sale. We were thinking about checking it out. Would that be okay if we incorporated a visit to see it while we're there?"

"Of course. Who knows, maybe I'll check out the area as well. It would be nice to live close to you. I mean, I've grown used to your breakfasts. If I do resettle in your vicinity, can I come over for my morning meal—like every day?"

"Of course, but wait. You've decided to move to the area when you get out?" Beth's voice reflected the excitement on her face.

"Not sure yet. I can't afford to live in Hawaii and besides, I have no real friends there. I don't know a lot about the area you're looking to move to, but there's tons of nursing jobs in this region. You know, coming back here to visit reminded me I do have roots." Selena took in her friend's happy smile. "And family."

"Aww. I'm glad God brought you back here so we could reconnect."

A peace filled Selena's soul. "So am I."

A man's face suddenly flashed before her and a voice whispered in her ear. *"Isn't he the real reason you came back?"* Selena turned, but there was no one there.

Chapter Eight

Beth popped open the rear gate and raised the glass. Anderson quickly grabbed the cooler while Beth removed the picnic basket. Selena retrieved the bag she had brought along. After walking into one of the pavilions, it only took a few seconds for the married couple to cover and set the table. Beth and Selena quickly dished out the food.

Anderson held up the Styrofoam bowl of fresh salad as he inspected the contents. "Is that pineapple I see in here?"

"Yes," Beth answered. "Selena and I made the food together. You'll find a touch of the islands in not only the garden salad, but also in the bread and Selena's potato salad."

"You made potato salad?" Reed asked "That's my mom's signature dish. I can't wait to find out what's in your recipe."

Beth caught the look of pride on Selena's face. All morning, Reed had been sending little compliments Selena's way.

Selena took a swig of her bottled water before responding. "One of the other nurses in my unit gave me this version. You might notice a hint of mint and coconut. I also made guava sweet bread for dessert."

"Wow, I can't wait to try it." Reed opened his sandwich. "Oh man, this smells heavenly. Cool. You made chicken salad, too? Can I have seconds?"

Color entered the corner of Selena's face, along with a smile. "Mango chicken salad and yes, we packed extra sandwiches for everyone." Selena glanced at the married couple. "Who is going to say grace?"

"Let me, please." Beth offered her hands and the four of them bowed their heads. "Gracious Father, we stand in awe of the majesty of the world You created. Thank You for designing such a wonderful creation full of the splendor of nature. We are also grateful for the bounty of blessings before us today. We ask your grace not only on the meal, but also on the friends around the table. Help the food nourish our bodies, and more importantly, remind us to cherish the bonds of friendship you've placed in our hearts. Amen."

Beth couldn't help but notice the look on Reed's face. His eyes were set on Selena. "Reed, thanks for coming along today. Did you enjoy the hike?"

He finished chewing before responding. "You know, I thought I was in great shape before I met Selly. It seems every time we get together, we take these long jaunts everywhere. I'm not sure if she's trying to impress me, build my endurance or push me to the breaking point. I wouldn't be surprised if she egged me on until I collapse."

Anderson and Beth both laughed. Selena took a long sip of her water. Beth knew her friend well enough to know she was searching for a humorous response. Beth beat her to it. "Well, consider yourself a lucky man if that does happen. I hear she's a terrific nurse."

"That's right," Anderson piped up. "Selena's got great first-aid skills. She patched me up when I tripped and cut my leg when we were hiking at Muddy Run."

Beth quickly shot her friend a wink. "And if the worst happens, I bet she's good at mouth-to-mouth resuscitation, aren't you, *Selly*?"

Selena couldn't help but snicker. "Some friend *you* are."

Reed touched Selena's arm. "Aren't friends great? They tease and pick on you, yet are always there when you need them. Take Trey for example. He's been my best friend since elementary school. No person in the entire world has joked with me nearly as much as he has. Always doing something to get the better of me."

Beth observed how Selena's face blanched. She removed Reed's fingers from her arm. "What do you mean?"

"Well, I bought this old Mustang GT when I got out of high school. Really hot car. The building Trey rented for the business was close to Franklin and Marshall College. A number of cute coeds lived in the house next door. I loved to burn rubber in the adjacent parking lot. I thought it impressed the ladies. They used to watch and wave at me when I'd tear out."

The nurse now rested her head on the palm of her hand. "So, you believed they thought you were cool, huh?"

"I was convinced they were enamored."

"You were most likely the butt of their jokes."

"I've matured enough to understand that, now." Reed raised his eyebrows. "May I finish?"

"Please do."

It was obvious that there was a growing connection between her friend and the plumber. Glancing at Anderson, Beth caught the smile that was also on his lips.

"Well, Trey teased me about it, unmercifully," Reed continued. "The more he did, the longer I'd squeal the wheels. And I'll admit, there was one girl in particular I was interested in showing off to. She had beautiful green eyes and long flowing blonde hair…"

Cocking her head, Selena interjected, "In case you were wondering… it's not really hip to go on and on about old girlfriends when you're on a date. Is the story about your car or the girl?"

"Sorry. It's actually about what Trey did to me."

"Can you fast forward to the funny part?"

Beth laughed out loud when Reed rolled his eyes. "Fine. One evening, the ladies next door were all outside, having a party. I hopped in my car and fired up the engine, revving it loudly. The women all ran to the fence to watch me. I slammed the transmission in gear, floored the gas pedal and popped the clutch."

Anderson, who owned a muscle car, was obviously interested. "What happened?"

"Nothing," Reed laughed. "The engine roared but the car didn't move. No squealing wheels, no burnt rubber, *nada*."

Selena was trying to restrain a giggle. "Why?"

"It seems my buddy, Trey, had jacked my car up while I was out on service calls. He put blocks under the axles so my tires were just off the ground."

The other three adults roared. Reed nodded. "Same reaction the girls had. But the incident did have a happy ending. I got a date with that girl I liked."

"Um-hmm. You were a lady's man back then as well. Much like today."

"If you're talking about how I managed to get the pretty girl to go out with me then, and the even prettier one to accompany me today... then I guess you're right."

Selena shook her head. "Flattery will get you nowhere. You forget, I've been surrounded by lovesick soldiers for years. There's no pick-up line I haven't heard. It's going take more than words to impress me."

Reed grew silent but suddenly clutched his chest and leaned forward.

Selena immediately jumped off the bench and started barking questions at him. "What's going on? Are you having chest pain? Are you allergic to something we ate? Did a bee sting you?"

Reed laid down on the bench, face to the sky. Selena dropped to her knees and grasped his arm. "Talk to me, Reed. What's your pain level?" One hand was on his wrist to take his pulse. The other fumbled to remove the cell from her pocket.

The man swiveled his head to face her. With a chuckle, he answered, "That depends."

Selena stopped and stared at him in astonishment. "What do you mean?"

"What level of pain do I need to have before you give me mouth-to-mouth?"

Selena's face turned pink, just before she shoved him off of the bench and under the table. "Jerk! Don't you ever pull that stunt again! Do you hear me?"

Reed was laughing now. "You said I had to find a unique way to get your attention."

Despite the anger in her friend's eyes, Beth could see the smile tugging at Selena's lips. "You are going to have to make this up to me."

"Obviously, that was my intention. How about dinner this evening?"

"If you live that long."

"Stop it. It was all in fun. I'm perfectly healthy."

"For the moment."

"What's that mean?"

"You like to joke, do you? Two can play at that game."

"Ooh, I love a challenge."

Selena shot a humorous look at Beth and then winked. "You heard him say it. At least I have witnesses on my side." She waited until Reed stood up before staring into his eyes. There was a smile on her lips when she told him, "So you want to tease? Game's on."

***

"Turn right at the next crossing." Beth slowed down and followed the instructions her husband was giving her. "We should see the lane in about six hundred feet." An old farmhouse sat on the left side of the road, directly across from the entrance. On the right, a worn gravel path all but disappeared into the partially wooded lot with quite a few weeds growing in the ruts.

Beth stopped her Explorer. "Is this it?" Glancing out the window, she noted For Sale signs on both sides of the road. "Is that house part of the property?"

Anderson shrugged. "I'm not quite sure. Let me go scan the QR code on this sign."

The four adults stepped from the SUV. After capturing the image, Beth's husband studied his phone. "It says the buildings are secluded from the road, so I'm assuming that house over there is a different property. Give me a few seconds." Anderson walked across the pavement and repeated the process on the other sign.

While she waited for her husband to return, Beth took in the old house. It had a certain charm to it, but it wasn't quite what the married couple had in mind.

Anderson called to her. "No. This one isn't part of the farmette. It's a different property. Let's follow the path and see where this trail leads."

A refreshing warm scent filled the air. It took a few seconds for Beth to identify the source. A thorny hedge ten or so yards from the path was filled with red raspberries. "Do you mind if we walk the rest of the way?"

"Of course not, honey." The comforting warmth of Anderson's hand added beauty to the late afternoon. Selena and Reed followed.

After fifty yards or so, the lane pivoted sharply to the left and followed the rise of the land. Twenty yards later, and after another turn, they caught a glimpse of several buildings. A large stone barn with a worn shingled roof dominated the grouping. A tractor shed leaned precariously against a tall walnut tree. Two other outbuildings appeared to be in desperate need of reinforcement just to remain standing.

They stopped in front of the large house. Built on the side of the hill, the remnants of a wrap-around porch sagged and major pieces of railing were missing. Large holes in the roof hinted at the damage waiting inside. What must have at one time been a patio lay dejectedly on the north side of the old homestead, looking over a small pond.

Silently, the four friends took it all in. Selena's voice broke the silence. "This place needs a lot of work."

Anderson slowly answered, "Yes, but it has quite a bit of potential. It must have been elegant in its heyday. The barn is salvageable, but I'm afraid the other buildings are too far gone. And the house? I'm not sure whether it can be saved. What do you think, Beth?"

It was a few moments before she answered. Yes, Anderson's assessment was correct, but there was more here. Her mind drifted not only to what it was in its current state, but also what it could be in the future. "What a beautiful home it must have been." She pointed to the pond. "I bet they had kids who chased frogs and hunted crayfish in the water." Next, she directed her attention to a briar patch just up the hill. "I can picture the lady of the house holding tea parties in the grape arbor. And the flower gardens surrounding the foundation must have been beautiful. It's so peaceful back here." She turned to the man who shared her name. "What do you envision?"

His blue eyes burned brightly as he held her and took it all in. "I can picture a sunroom facing the pond, with a fireplace, of course. A haven for you and I to sip our morning cup of coffee while we watch the deer frolic in the grass by our little pond." Anderson touched the side of Beth's face so they were looking into each other's eyes. "I can see us raising our family here, with enough room for our children to run and play and explore. And later on, when they're gone, I see us sitting on a swing under a million stars, dreaming of forever. What I see when I take in the old place is a home to share for a lifetime—for you and me."

Anderson then grew quiet. Beth asked the obvious. "This is the one we've been waiting for, isn't it?"

He nodded. "I think so."

Reed's voice interrupted the trance. "There's still an awful lot of work to make this place livable. And it's so far from Lancaster. Would you really even consider living here?"

The married couple didn't even glance in his direction when they answered as one. "Yes."

Chapter Nine

"Are you looking forward to heading back to the islands?"

Selena shook her head. "I'm not happily anticipating leaving the Army. But as soon as I pack my belongings, I'll be coming back. It was a nice place to be stationed, but Hawaii is not my home."

Beth sat on the bed as Selena worked on packing her things. "I can still make arrangements to come with you if you want me to."

This task would be even harder than she had anticipated. Thankfully she had Beth's friendship to lean on. "Maybe someday we can all take in Hawaii when we're on vacation."

"Will you be inviting Reed to come along?"

A smile crept to her lips as the man's face appeared in her mind. "We'll have to see where God leads me. I didn't tell you, but he also volunteered to join me."

"He's probably looking forward to some mouth-to-mouth, you know, if he can't breathe."

"He's been hinting about that first kiss since the trip to Caledonia."

"What he did was funny."

Selena shook her head. "And a little scary. I thought for a second he was serious."

"I bet he won't do that again."

"No, he wouldn't dare. He's a good guy. I'm going to miss him."

"Will he be waiting when you return?"

"I hope so." She stopped and turned to face her friend. "Thanks for your friendship. It feels like we picked up right where we left off. As if we truly are sisters."

Beth touched her arm. "That's because we are and always will be. And a chosen sister is the very best kind. So, when you get back to Lancaster, what's next? Have you made a decision as to where you'll plant roots?"

Selena had a plan but hadn't shared it with anyone, yet. She was waiting to hear back on her offer. "I'm not sure, but I just know it won't be Hawaii."

"Well, I for one am hoping it will be somewhere close to this area."

Selena noted how Beth glanced at her phone when it vibrated. "Everything okay?"

"Oh, it's just Andy telling me he's going to be a little late tonight, that's all."

"We can change our dinner reservations, if that works." Selena had offered to take the pair out to dinner as a thank you.

Beth's face had a tinge of pink. "I've got an idea. What would you think of going over to the tea room, you know, to celebrate our friendship?"

Selena zipped up her duffle bag. She was all packed and prepared for her flight the following morning. "On the way over, you can tell me about the new property."

"Great. I'll meet you in the car. I'll drive, if you don't mind."

Selena shook her head as she watched Beth walk off the porch. The younger woman sported a different pair of cheap sunglasses and yet another of her signature, floppy hats. This one matched the yellow top she wore. Beth was smiling. "Ready?"

"Yep." They climbed into the SUV. "When do you settle on the property?"

"At the end of the month. Andy and I sketched out our plans for the house. We'll start shopping for a contractor after settlement."

"This has to be so exciting for you."

Beth hesitated. "Yes, and no. We've dreamed about this for so long, but now that it's actually happening, I'm more than a little scared."

"About what?"

"Going into debt has me concerned."

"Debt is a part of life. Haven't you ever had a car payment?"

"Duh! I drive a fifteen-year-old Ford that has two hundred thousand miles on it."

"But I thought you two had a big down payment set aside."

Beth turned the wheel to head in the direction of the establishment. "We do, but we decided to have a new house built on the property."

"A brand new one? Can you afford it?"

"Yes. It's just that I've never borrowed money before. Plus, now that it's happening, I'm having second thoughts about moving so far away from my family... to be honest, from my mom."

Selena laughed. "They're only an hour or so away. It's not like they live in Hawaii."

"I know, but still, I'm used to being able to visit whenever I want to. Knowing if I needed something, Mom or Sam would be there in a matter of minutes. It was a comforting feeling."

Selena looked out the window so Beth wouldn't see the smile on her face. "Guess you'll just have to get used to being in the wilderness of South Mountain, all alone..."

The Explorer rolled to a stop. "You're right. Hey look, we're here."

The parking lot looked fuller than normal for mid-afternoon. It might have been her imagination, but Selena could have sworn some of the cars were familiar. "Is that Andy's car over there?"

Beth popped the rear lid and removed a bag. "Why would his car be here if he's working late?"

A tingling feeling walked across Selena's shoulder. "What's in the bag?"

"I, uh, borrowed something from Sophie Miller. I'm just returning it."

Something's not right here. "You live next to the Millers. Why not just drop it off at her house instead?"

"Umm, Sophie asked me to bring it here."

"Bethany Warren... are you telling me the truth?"

Her friend's face was now totally pink. "Do you doubt me?"

"Yes, I do. Something's going on. Did you plan a party?"

Beth shook her head. "I swear on a stack of Bibles I did not plan one. Why? Did you want a party?"

Selena could tell by Beth's expression that her friend was telling the truth. "No. I'm sorry for ever doubting you."

Threading her arm into Selena's, Beth joked, "Of course, all bets are off when you return."

"Thanks for the warning."

The bell on the door tinkled as it opened. Sophie Miller was perched on her seat inside the door and greeted them in her usual British accent. The short blonde reached for the bag Beth carried. "I'll take care of that for you. Thanks." She led them to the back room with Selena bringing up the rear.

As soon as Selena entered, she was met with a shout. "Surprise!" A quick glance around revealed a number of friendly faces, including Beth's family, husband and Selena's grandmother.

Whipping to face Beth, she was met with laughter. "It wasn't me—I told you the truth. I did not set this up."

"Then who did?"

Beth pointed to Selena's right. "She did."

Selena pivoted to find the smiling face of Rose Sheppard.

***

"I don't understand why you are planning this party for Selena."

Trey watched her eyes as the lady looked up from her computer. "Because I like doing nice things for others."

"I see, but why Selena?"

"Selly is going through a tough time right now. Imagine how hard it is for her, losing her job and trying to decide what's next. Yet, through it all, she's maintained her kindness. I can feel God's spirit moving in her life."

"This is generous of you, but I still don't understand why you have such an interest in her."

Rose touched his hand gently. "You two were close friends. Any friend of yours is a friend of mine."

"That was years ago and besides, you know we were more than friends. Doesn't that bother you in the least?"

"Do you still feel the same way about her?"

The blue in Rose's eyes was so bright this morning. A warmth rose in Trey's chest. "You know the answer to that question."

"But at one time, Selly was someone very special to you. In my experience, once love begins, it never truly dies. On some level she still matters to you. And Trey, what is important to you means the same to me."

"When did you become a philosopher?"

"I may have taken a couple of courses in that subject at Millersville, but I'm no philosopher."

"That's right. I forgot you had a bachelor's degree."

"Plus a master's degree in business from Elizabethtown College."

"Guess I forgot about your MBA." Somewhere deep in his brain, a thought came to life. "With all your education, why did you ever take a job managing this business?"

"Haven't you figured that out yet?"

He shook his head.

"Because you were here."

***

Trey sat at the table, sipping his iced tea. He was only at the party because Rose asked him to accompany her. In the last couple of weeks, he'd found it increasingly difficult to say no to her for any reason. That was why he was sitting in the back room of Sophie Miller's tea room. His only task had been to carry in the box of supplies Rose and her sister had assembled. His friend Reed was also here, but Reed was happily assisting with the decorations.

Ever one for working safely, Reed used the short ladder he'd brought along. He held one side of the banner up against the wall. "Is this where you want it?"

Rose backed away so she could check it out, but Lily was the one who answered. "Shift it a little more to the left. Yeah, that looks good. Come over here and help me hang the balloons, please." Lily grabbed the decorations from Rose's hand and headed to the far side.

Trey caught the expression on Rose's face. Now that he was spending time with the Sheppard twins, he could detect a delicate undercurrent between them.

He grabbed Rose's glass and walked to her. "You look parched. Want something to drink?"

A smile wiped away her previous frustration. "Thank you."

"Your sister seems to love being in charge."

"One of Lily's many qualities is organization."

"And the desire to be in control."

Rose shifted so she could fully see his face. "Every one of us has flaws. I certainly have mine."

He studied her, but didn't respond.

Her eyes begged the question, "What are you thinking?"

A little laugh escaped him. "I've yet to notice a single one of yours."

Rose now looked away, her cheeks pink. "As time goes on, you'll find each and every one of them, I'm sure. And there's plenty."

"I highly doubt that, but if what you say is true, it won't matter. I'm beginning to believe you are perfect. Know why?"

Trey would have had to be blind not to notice the affection on her face as she shook her head.

"That's because I see you through... are you ready?" She nodded. "*Rose*-colored glasses."

They both giggled. He had never seen anyone as beautiful before. It was time. He moved to kiss her. Rose tilted her head and was just about to meet his lips when Lily called out, "Trey, can you give Reed a hand here?"

Before he could respond, Rose turned away. There was nothing to do but assist in the tasks Lily assigned him.

Guests began to arrive moments later. Since she had arranged the party, Rose greeted each one and thanked them for coming. His girl paid special attention to Selena's grandmother, Esther, placing her next to where Selena would be seated.

Trey was so engrossed in watching Rose, he didn't notice the person who dropped into the seat next to him. The warm touch on his skin almost startled him. It was Lily. She had taken his hand. "My sister is pretty cool, isn't she?"

There was something a little unnerving about Rose's sister, but he hadn't yet figured out exactly what it was. Trey turned to face her. "Looks like a good turnout, doesn't it?"

The girl took a sip of tea before responding. "Yep. Once again, my older sister has put together an excellent celebration."

"She did. Your sister is very special."

Lily sighed, offering a frown. "I know. I've heard that every day since we were born. And when people compare us, Rose is always the favorite. It's tough always coming in second to my twin."

"Life's not a competition between the two of you. You've got lots of things going for you. Just be yourself and don't compare yourself to Rose."

"Regardless, everyone always does that and without fail, picks my sister over me. Just once, I'd like to be the best."

"One day, you'll find someone who feels that way about you."

Her hand trembled against his arm. "Trey, would you ever consider..."

Before he could answer, Reed whispered loudly, "Shh. Here she comes. Quiet, everybody."

Lily slipped away to take her place next to Rose. The trio of women appeared—first, Sophie Miller, then Beth and finally Selena. Everyone yelled, "Surprise!" when the lady of the hour entered the room. Trey took it all in as Rose led Selena from guest to guest, of course, with Lily in tow.

Trey sat at the very rear table, which provided an excellent place to watch and think. While Selena's face had thinned and her hair was shorter, she was still quite attractive. His mind drifted back in time... to the day he'd met her.

It had been the first day of his sophomore year in high school. He'd been in the hallway heading to algebra when someone ran into the girl in front of him. Her books fell all over the floor. Instinctively, Trey grabbed a few and handed them back. But when she turned to take them from him, he'd stood in awe. She was pretty, but that wasn't why. Instead, there was something else about her that touched him inside—in a way he'd never felt before. As if he'd just met his future. She must not have noticed because after thanking him, she simply walked away.

A round of laughter interrupted his daydream, but only for a second. All that first month of school, everywhere he went, he'd seen her. It had taken a lot of courage to introduce himself. Closing his eyes, he remembered the beauty of her face and the sound of her voice saying his name.

"Hello, Trey."

He forced off the thought and found himself face to face with the girl he once loved. The one he'd promised to spend his life with. The girl he'd thrown away. Her hand was extended in front of him. After the vision, his mind and heart argued over whether to shake her hand or wrap his arms around her and beg forgiveness.

"Hello. Are you in there?"

His body, held captive by the internal argument, finally freed itself. He took Selena's hand. "Sorry. It's good to see you again. I understand you're leaving? Rose told me the Army is letting you go. I'm sorry about that. I know that was your dream, to follow your mom's footsteps."

Selena's lips pinched together like she was struggling for control. "I did achieve my dream. Well, most of it."

That puzzled him. "I don't understand."

"Mom was more than a nurse. She was a wonderful mother and devoted wife who married the man of her dreams."

Man of her dreams? That was what Selena used to call him. The sentence sank in, bringing the guilt of what he'd done to her a decade ago.

Out of the corner of his eye, he watched as Rose stepped away, dragging Lily with her. His girl was giving him space. "I'm sorry, Selena. I know I hurt you. There was nothing else I could have done."

A frown now appeared. "I don't believe that for a second, but... that's all in the past. It looks like you are well on your way to finding *your* happiness. Rose is a wonderful lady, and she loves you, Trey. Thanks for coming today and well... good luck in all you do." She kissed his cheek, quickly wiped her eyes and put a smile on her face before heading for her seat in the front of the room.

Rose followed Selena and made a couple of announcements. His heart was shaken by the unexpected suddenness and depth of the feeling in his soul. Despite the brevity of their conversation, Selena's comment had spoken volumes. The argument raged full bore in his mind.

Could I have handled things differently?

Idiot! You know the answer. Was it really necessary to break her heart the way you did?

But Selena might have given up her dream if I hadn't done it. It was all for her own good.

Is that what really happened?

Of course. I had to consider her future.

Aren't you the White Knight? Sacrificing a love that was real just so you would feel better. All because of your home situation.

What do you mean?

Oh, look at me. Poor pitiful me. I've got to stay home and take care of everyone else. Look how humble I am. What I gave up for the sake of others.

"Stop this."

"Are you talking to me?"

Trey turned to find Lily next to him. "No, I'm sorry. I was talking to myself."

There was a hurt look on the girl's face. "You know, Rose and I might not get along one hundred percent of the time, but she's my sister and I love her. So let me tell you this, Trey Brubaker..." She stepped closer until he could feel her breath against his face. Her voice dropped to a hissed whisper. "If you break my sister's heart over Selena Harper... you *will* answer to me."

Chapter Ten

"Hi, Selena. How are you?"

"Not too well. Got a few minutes?"

Selena was standing all alone on the sand at Ka'a'awa Beach Park on the North Shore of Oahu. She'd taken a drive to clear her mind and had decided this was as good of a place as any to stop.

Beth's voice was a balm to her ears. "I've always got time for you. What's going on?"

"Such drama in my life. Just as I was ready to muster out, the Army offered me another post."

"Really? Where?"

"Okinawa."

"Where's that?"

"It's one of the Japanese islands in the Pacific. About eight thousand miles from home. I was there for three days on my way to Korea a couple of years ago."

There was a delay. "Are you going?"

The crash of the waves momentarily caught Selena's attention. "If I stay in the service, life would be simpler."

"Then I guess congratulations are in order. When do you report to your new duty station?"

"That's the issue. I'm not sure if I want to go."

"Hold on a second." In the background, Selena heard Beth ask for a specific kind of whoopie pie. That meant she was probably at her mother's home for a meal.

"Sorry, this is a bad time for you. Tell your mom I said hello. I'll hang up now."

"No, no. I just wanted to get my order in before my little sisters take all the best treats."

On the other end of the line, the distinctive sound of a screen door slamming was evident. That meant Beth was outside on the porch at her mother's place. The squeak of the springs on the old glider brought back memories. "You're sitting on the swing on the front porch, aren't you?"

"How did you guess?"

"You and I used to hang out there, remember? Good memories of a simpler time."

"That they were. Okay, I'm situated. What's on your mind?"

"Where you are."

"Come again?"

The waves were picturesque this morning. A few surfers were trying them out. "I miss home."

"Home? You mean like in Lancaster?"

"Not just the place, but the people who are my real and virtual family. You, Andy, my grandmom, your family, even the Sheppard twins. The whole slew of them. After spending last month surrounded by these people, I'm not sure I want to return to Army life. It was much easier when the brass decided my service was no longer needed. But now, at the eleventh hour, they granted me a reprieve."

"Will you take it?"

Selena slipped off her shoes and socks and rubbed her feet in the sand, watching the grains filter in between her toes. "Part of me wants to stay in the service, but then another part says no... that it's time to plant roots. Time to begin really living. I'm so envious of you. What I'd give for a life like you and Andy share. One with dreams and plans... and a future together. It would be wonderful to be surrounded by people who care, and I mean really care for and about me."

Beth's laugh seemed out of place. "When can we expect you?"

"For what?"

"To come back here. I think you called to have an empathetic ear, which is me. But as I listen to you, I know you well enough to understand... you've already made your mind up."

"But that's just it. I haven't. That's why I wanted to hear your thoughts, to help me decide what I should do. Part of me wants to continue my career, yet inside, I yearn for what was all around me when I was on leave. I've been a loner for years, but all that changed last month."

Her friend's voice was soft. "What you felt was the love of family. Maybe not by blood, but by choice. And it won't matter where you go, we'll always be here."

"Then you think I should go to Okinawa?"

"That's not what I said. What I meant was that in the past, our friendship withered. I won't let that happen again. All of us really enjoyed you being here. But for you and me, it was like when we were kids—BFFs and all that stuff." Selena could almost feel Beth's sigh. "One thing I've learned in life is to never pass up on the opportunity to tell others how you feel. You're like a sister to me. I'd love to have you live close by, so we could raise our families together. But I know you also have dreams, and I want them to come true."

"I still don't understand what you mean. What do you think I should do?"

"I can't make the decision for you. But what I am saying is that when you decide to return, whether that's now or later or maybe never, I'll be here. You have a family now. One that loves you. That will never end."

The blue ocean was blurry. "I had it all planned out. I wanted to plant roots there. I even picked out a place to live. But I never expected the Army to offer me another chance."

"Yet, they did. What are you going to do?"

"I'm not really sure. I was hoping you would help me decide."

Again, Beth laughed. "What you mean is that you wanted me to decide for you."

"Well, if you put it that way, yes—something like that."

"Sorry, but I won't do that. You are, how did Rose's sister put it... oh yeah, you're at a critical crossroad in life's journey. Only you can decide the path to take. Back into the service will help fulfill your dreams, but leaving offers a different journey with other rewards. Only you can decide the path for your life."

Selena shook her head. "Too bad it's not like her sister Rose says and that God already has it all picked out for me. Then, I would simply need to follow the road He leads me down."

"Amen. There you go, sister. Maybe that's what He's done. Now, what's it going to be?"

"I don't know. Since you won't assist me, maybe I'll just stay here on the beach, under fair trade winds and sunny skies while I wait for divine intervention."

"Now I'm the envious one. Seriously, let me know what you decide. If you do come back, give me fair warning so I can plan the party."

"Yeah, right. Goodbye and tell everyone I said hello."

"Peace be with you. Talk to you soon."

Selena tossed the cell on the bench. It was beautiful on this island. And Okinawa would be equally as enchanting, but still...

God, I'm seeking your guidance. You know my heart, my dreams, my desires. Guide my soul and help me make the best decision. The breeze suddenly ruffled her hair, but was it just the trade winds... or the finger of God?

***

"I don't think you've said two words to me all evening. What's on your mind?"

Trey glanced up, taking in Rose's blue eyes. "Nothing, really."

Rose sighed, deeply. "It was nice of you to take me out to dinner, but maybe there were other things you would rather do. And I'm not only talking about tonight. You've been like this for the last month. I'm beginning to think you've grown tired of being with me."

I've got to get out of this funk. "That's not the case at all."

"Then what's going on?"

"I don't know. Maybe it's the stress of everything I've got going on in my life. I'm trying to help my mom find a new car and working with my sister on her college algebra. She's in danger of failing. And there's so much to do with the business. I guess all those things are adding up."

Rose picked at her salad with her fork. "But those challenges have been constant in your life since I met you."

"That's not true. Take the car for example..." He paused when he noted Rose's raised finger. "What?"

"I wasn't speaking specifically of the current individual tasks. Look at the bigger picture. Helping your family has always been a prime concern for you and I admire that. It's one of the many reasons I feel like I do about you. But you've never been this down before. Why is that?"

I can't admit it. "I don't know. Look, can we change the subject?"

Those pretty blue eyes were tinged with sadness. "Please be honest with me, Trey."

"I am." *No, you're lying to her.*

"And despite my plea, the man remains silent." Rose pushed her plate to the center of the table and wiped her napkin across her mouth. The words she spoke were deliberate and measured. "In First Corinthians, God made His expectations clear concerning true and deep relationships between a man and a woman. He expects open and honest communication. He wants them to be helpmates to each other. He stated that while they are two bodies, they'll be of one spirit."

Trey took a sip of water, but it was hard to get it down his throat. "He was talking about a married couple, wasn't He?"

"Yes, but let's be honest. I truly believed the first time I met you that you were the one God made for me. I've been in love with you since the first day I saw you. I've waited and waited for you to open your eyes to my feelings and what was right in front of you. I thought you finally had. But the bitter truth stands before me. I've been wrong, all along. I made a major mistake."

"What? No, that isn't true."

Rose opened her purse and placed a few bills on the table. Her hands were trembling and her cheeks wet. "Thank you for a nice evening, but it's time for me to leave."

This can't be happening. "You haven't even finished your dinner."

"I'm not hungry."

"Let me drive you home."

"That's okay. I'll give Lily a call. She'll gladly pick me up."

"But Rose..."

She stood before him. As if in slow motion, Rose bent down and kissed him full on the lips. Trey began to wrap his arms around her, but Rose pushed them away. She stood and searched his eyes. "Sorry, but I had to do that, just one time. This is goodbye, Trey."

In disbelief, Trey watched Rose Sheppard walk away.

Chapter Eleven

His mother's old Impala had failed to start, yet again, so he'd had to rearrange his schedule and drive her to work. In Trey's haste to pick her up, he'd run a stop sign and now had an expensive citation as a memento. The topping on the morning had been the safe driving lecture his mother had provided following the ticket, all the way to her work. "What a day." And it wasn't even ten.

But the thing weighing heaviest on his mind was Rose. He'd waited a few minutes after her hasty departure from the restaurant before trying to call, but his efforts all went to voicemail. In desperation, he'd driven to her home. Then, when he knocked, it wasn't Rose, but her father who had answered. The look of anger on the older man's face couldn't be missed.

"Mr. Brubaker, how can I help you?"

"Good evening, Mr. Sheppard. I was hoping to speak to your daughter."

The old man had jammed his finger in Trey's chest so hard that it hurt. *"I knew you were trouble from the second I met you. And let me tell you something..."*

"Daddy, let me handle this." Trey had turned, hoping to find Rose, but instead, Lily stood there.

The man swung around, angry, but a whisper-quiet conversation took place, then Mr. Sheppard abruptly stormed off.

Lily stepped forward and said nothing, but stared at him with an incensed expression.

"I need to see Rose."

"No. That will not happen."

"I need to know she's okay."

The fire in Lily's eyes could have ignited a whole forest of wet pines. *"My sister and her wellbeing are no longer your concern."*

"Please, I, I, uh, I don't know what went wrong, but I need to talk to her. I want to make this right. I want to tell her what she means to me."

Her slap was not anticipated. Lily's finger was right in his face. *"Selena Harper, that's what went wrong. I told you before that if you hurt my sister, you'd have to deal with me."* Lily shoved him backwards and started to close the door, but instead, pulled it open again. *"Not only did Rose misjudge you, but I did as well. I thought you were so nice and that Rose was right—you were the man of her dreams. But both of our eyes are open, now. You're the world's biggest fool and I hope I never have to lay eyes on you again. May you rot in Hades for hurting my sister."*

With her diatribe complete, Lily slammed the door in his face. Head down, he'd walked to the street. As he opened his car door, Trey took one last look at the house. He couldn't be sure, but Trey could have sworn on his life that he caught a glimpse of Rose watching him from one of the upstairs windows.

***

Trey finally arrived at work. A quick glance at the cars in the parking lot confirmed his suspicion. Rose's vehicle was missing. *Par for the course. I need to talk to her, but how?* Wait! Reed had all the answers about Rose, so maybe he'd know where to find her.

He rushed through the office and directly into the shop. But when he got to the Service Desk, Reed wasn't there. Trey called out, but there was no one at all in the shop. Ripping his cell from his pocket, he dialed his friend, but it went directly to voicemail.

"Great. What else can go wrong?" Trey returned to his desk, hoping to have a moment to think clearly. That was when he saw it. A pink envelope rested in the exact center of his desk. Trey noticed that it had been opened, even though it was addressed to him.

Trey's hands were shaking as he pulled the sheet out of the envelope. After reading it, he released the paper. Just then, the air conditioning fan kicked on and the note fluttered off the desk and into the waste paper basket. The comparison to his own life wasn't lost on him.

***

Reed was in a bad slump. Selena had told him about the Army's offer a couple of weeks ago. But the poor girl hadn't yet made up her mind. She chose to remain in Hawaii while she tried to make a decision. The situation had come to a head over the weekend. Because Selena was dragging her feet about the future, Reed stupidly suspected there might be another man involved. Then, like the fool he was, he'd confronted her about his thoughts. She promptly denied the accusation. It was a mistake he now regretted, but Reed had lost his temper. He insisted it was time for her to quit the Army and get back to Lancaster, immediately. After all, Reed was waiting. *Nice incentive, right? What a gem I am.*

The words had no sooner escaped his lips when she disconnected. And every call he made to her now dumped directly to voicemail, none of which she had returned. He had messed up, royally. What should he do? While he might not have a clue, there was someone who would. The person he considered the smartest woman in the world—Rose.

Reed made sure he was at work extra early so he'd be able to speak to his friend. He and Rose had drawn close in the two years she'd worked there. If not for the massive attachment she had to Trey, and his respect for both of those friends, Reed would have pulled out all the stops to win Rose's heart. Since he knew a romantic relationship was out of the question, he had to settle for a close friendship instead.

Reed had even stopped to buy her a coffee, but was surprised when she wasn't at her desk. Disappointed, he placed the cup on Rose's blotter and headed to the shop. Maybe he'd catch her after getting the shift started.

Down a man, Reed had assisted one of the plumbers in pulling supplies for a job at a livestock barn. It was after nine when he walked back into the office. Much to his surprise, neither Trey nor Rose were there. *Bet the lucky guy took her out for breakfast.*

Reed was about to return to the shop when he noticed Rose's prized autographed photo of Tom Brady was missing. Walking over to her desk, he found it wasn't just the photo that was missing—all of her personal items were gone. *But they were all there this morning.* Yet the cup of coffee he'd bought for her sat untouched.

Quickly glancing at Trey's desk, Reed noticed a pink envelope. Rushing over, he saw it was addressed to Trey, but the handwriting undoubtedly belonged to Rose. Without a second thought, he ripped open the covering and read the contents. After replacing the paper and returning the envelope to exactly where he'd found it, he tried to call Rose. When his call bounced to voicemail, Reed assumed she had turned the device off.

"Think, think, where would she go?" He had suspicions as to her whereabouts and followed his instincts by pointing his car in that direction. But Reed also did his due diligence, just in case. A quick phone call to the Sheppard home went unanswered. Luckily, he knew enough about Rose's life to know where her mother worked.

Reed breathed a sigh of relief when Rose's mom came on the line. "Hello?"

"Mrs. Sheppard, so sorry to bother you at the office. I know we've never met, but my name is Reed Thomas and I work with Rose. She's not at the shop and I believe something happened to her. I'm just trying to make sure she's okay."

The woman huffed before answering. "She and that Trey Brubaker broke up last night. My daughter tendered her resignation this morning."

"I don't mean to pry, but do you know where she went?"

"Not exactly. She packed a basket before she left, so I assume she wasn't planning on coming home for a while. Hopefully she's out job hunting. You know, I never thought she should have taken that stupid job in a plumbing shop. She was a manager in a big industrial plant..." The lady went on for another five minutes before saying goodbye. Reed used the time wisely and was almost in Chatham by the time her mother had hung up.

Twenty minutes later, Reed turned into the parking lot. He found Rose's car within five minutes. Running to the entrance of Longwood Gardens, he quickly purchased a ticket, grabbed a map and asked the clerk, "Which way to the Chimes Tower?"

The woman behind the counter grinned at him. "Are you in a hurry, sir?"

"Yes, yes. Which way to the tower?"

"May I ask why you're in a rush?"

"Because my closest friend in the world needs me and that's where I'll find her."

Chapter Twelve

Despite the beautiful location, Rose's spirit was broken. There was but one thing to do—pray for guidance. "I'm sorry, Lord. I thought I was following the plan You had for my life. But in retrospect, I realize instead it was only *my* pride and desire to have my own way. It wasn't Your will at all. Please forgive me, Lord. My heart is open to you, now. Please show me the path You've created for me."

Rose truly believed God answered every single prayer. So, she waited for His response, for the Lord to speak to her. After a while, the soothing sound of the waterfall lulled her into a deep meditation. The surroundings might be beautiful this morning, but she really didn't see them. A slight mist from the tumbling water touched her face. Birds of all kinds flitted here and there as peace settled on her soul. The serenity made her think that this place just might resemble the Garden of Eden, before the devil corrupted Adam and Eve... before Rose's desires tainted her life.

Closing her eyes, Rose drew a deep breath of air full of the essence of nature. Peace continued to coat her mind, until the slapping noise of running feet interrupted the calmness. Opening her eyes, a man with a familiar face ran toward her.

He was out of breath. "Rose, thank God, I found you."

"Reed? What are you doing here? How did you know where to find me?"

"Where else would you be? This is your favorite place in the whole world. I knew this is where you'd be." He sat next to her on the bench.

"But why are you here?"

"Because you're my best friend and I knew you'd need me."

Extracting a tissue from her purse, Rose wiped her eyes. "I should have known. How much did Trey tell you?"

"Trey? I haven't seen or spoken with him."

"Then, I don't understand why you're sitting next to me."

"I saw your desk had been cleaned out. I know it was wrong, but when I saw the envelope on Trey's desk, I panicked. In my heart, I knew something wasn't right. I knew you would want me to come."

A bad feeling climbed up her spine. "Please tell me you didn't read what was inside."

"Of course, I did. I needed to find out what happened... why you weren't at the shop."

"But that letter was personal. I addressed it to Trey. You had no right to read what I wrote."

Reed appeared to be in shock. "But Rose, I was worried about you. I knew having a friend would comfort you."

"I'm fine."

"But you quit your job, all because—"

For the first time in a long while, anger welled up inside her. "I cannot for the life of me understand why you had the audacity to read my letter. That note contained my personal feelings, of issues between Trey and me. Things that were never meant to be shared with anyone else, especially you."

"But I'm your best friend. I had a right to—"

Holding up the palm of her hand, she paused before continuing. "A right? What right? And where do you get this 'best friend' thing? Whether you're my friend or not, I am entitled to my privacy. Don't you agree?"

"Yes, but Trey doesn't care for you like I do. You even said in the letter that he cares more about Selena than—"

It took quite a bit of restraint to keep her cool. "Stop it. You want to help? Then quit attacking me. What was written on those pages was never meant to be read by you—or anyone else besides Trey. And I would appreciate that in the future you respect my privacy. Are we clear on that?"

He swallowed hard. "Yes, ma'am." Reed's expression was one of disbelief. They faced each other in silence for what felt like hours. When the carillon bells in the tower rang out, the trance was broken.

Finally closing her eyes, Rose pondered if she'd gone too far. While what Reed did was wrong, she'd also made a mistake of taking her anger at Trey out on Reed. "Look, maybe I came on a little too strong. It's just that, well, my day hasn't turned out like I'd hoped."

He shook his head and turned away from her. "I understand and I sincerely offer my apologies for interfering. I'm not sure if I just misunderstood things or maybe have everything all wrong in my head, but one thing is clear. It's time for me to go."

"You don't have to leave, but I still don't quite understand why you're even here."

He shifted his weight from one foot to the other. "I thought you needed one, so I was trying to be a good friend."

"And she has one... in me."

Now it was Rose's turn to be astounded. Trey Brubaker appeared from behind Reed, holding a bouquet of pink roses.

***

After retrieving Rose's letter from the garbage, Trey sat down to think. As he analyzed all that happened, he realized Rose was correct. Because of the funk he'd fallen into, he hadn't given her the attention she deserved.

At the farewell party, Selena's comment had struck a deep chord within him. Trey *could* have done things differently instead of falling on the sword of injustice the world had offered. In retrospect, breaking up was easier than working through the problem with Selena's assistance. But that was what he'd done and nothing could change it now.

His fingers traced across the pink page. In a few places, the ink was smudged and the paper was discolored. He knew what the spots were from—Rose's tears. Where they had fallen when she'd hand-written the letter with not only the termination of her employment, but her final goodbye.

Trey held the paper close and inhaled. The faint scent of her perfume was still present. It was quite clear now. While reaching for a bud that had once grown in his life, he'd overlooked the perfect flower that had fully bloomed right in front of him. The most beautiful and wonderful woman in the entire world—Rose. "What do I do now?"

Resolve suddenly filled his chest. "I am not going to let history repeat itself. I lost one woman I loved, but I won't let this happen again." Stuffing the message in his pocket, he ran out the door.

Trey knew that Longwood was where Rose went to think, meditate and pray. He believed that would be where he could find the woman this morning. Upon pulling into the lot, he also searched for her vehicle. Trey quickly found it and rushed to the gate. After stopping at the garden store, he then grabbed a map. Perusing it, he considered where Rose might be found. His first guess had been the Italian Water Gardens.

She wasn't there. His next notion was Rose might be in the Conservatory. Every time she'd brought him to the gardens, they had spent hours taking in the orchids. He was fast approaching the entrance of the big glass building when the chimes in the bell tower rang out. The sound brought his feet to a dead stop. Rose had shared how much she loved the tower and waterfall. If Rose was anywhere, she'd be at the foot of the falls.

Trey ran like a man possessed. *I've got to find her. I need to make this right.* Like an antelope running from a lioness, he took the stairs from the observation platform that overlooked the fountains three at a time. In the distance, he caught a glimpse of a golden-haired woman at the base of the falls. As he drew close, he noticed she was talking to someone. A person he knew well—Reed Thomas.

Trey stood behind his friend, just out of Rose's line of sight. When he heard Reed tell Rose he was trying to be a friend, Trey knew it was time.

Reed's back was to Trey as he spoke. "I thought you needed one, so I was trying to be a good friend."

Trey couldn't wait any longer. "And she has one... in me."

Trey stepped around so he could clearly see Rose. The girl's mouth hung open as she stared at him. "Trey?"

"Rose, we need to talk. You were right. I should have been completely honest with you and I never should have ignored you. Can we talk?"

He couldn't help but notice how Rose's hands were trembling. "Did you read the note?"

"Yes, and I don't want to accept either part of it—your resignation or our breakup. Is there still time to discuss this?"

Much to Trey's surprise, Reed stuck his foot in the conversation. After looking at both of them, he said, "Rose, why would you believe him? You saw first-hand how he's still attracted to Selena."

Trey's fists curled. Reed had been his best friend for years, but now the man was getting on his last nerve. He was about to lash out at him when Rose spoke.

"I know you're trying to be a friend, but this is none of your business, Reed. I'd like some privacy so I can speak with Trey. Would you pay both of us the common courtesy of giving us time alone?"

Over the years, Trey had seen Reed angry more than once. But right now, his friend's face couldn't get any redder if someone had thrown a gallon of candy apple red paint on it. And the way the veins stood out in his temples? The man's words hissed out of him like steam escaping a pipe leak. "Yes, ma'am. I know where I'm no longer wanted." Reed turned and stormed off into the afternoon sun. Trey watched him depart.

When the man was no longer visible, Trey turned to Rose. "Can we sit and talk?"

Rose nodded and led him to a bench. Sitting next to her, he could feel not only her eyes watching him, but her heart probing Trey's intentions. "You were completely right."

The girl brushed the hair from his eyes. "You still love her, don't you?"

"No."

Her finger was against his lips. "Please be totally honest with me."

He nodded slowly. "Okay. I promise. At the party, when I apologized to her for the past, Selena told me things could have been different. And she was right. I could have... no, should have handled everything differently. But instead, I broke her heart."

"And you still love her, don't you?"

It was hard to say the words, because they would seem different in the light of day. "I believe what you said is true. When you love someone, that love doesn't ever really end. It may not work out like you hope, but the part of your heart you gave away is never all yours again."

Trey paused when he saw Rose's eyes well. "I also accept as truth that God helps our hearts heal and grow anew. In our case, I've been waiting for the part of my heart I gave to Selena to grow back. It finally did, but there's just one problem."

She wiped a hand across her cheek. "Which is?"

"All of my heart now belongs to you."

"But your actions don't support that. She's always on your mind. I know you love Selena."

"Yes, I do… but in the past tense. Now… it is you I love—in the present tense. Please forgive me for not being honest with you. Can you give us another chance?"

Rose fought back a sob. "I want that more than anything."

He reached for her hands. She grasped his tightly. "Can you forgive me?"

"I forgave you long before you showed up here."

Dropping her hands, Trey wrapped his arms around her. "Thank you for coming into my life. You are the answer to my prayers."

"And I really hope you are the answer to mine."

Chapter Thirteen

Beth was applying the finishing touches on the cake when the phone rang. After placing the spatula on the counter, she licked the traces of the chocolate mixture from her fingers before reaching for her phone.

"Well look who it is. Selena Harper. You really do exist."

"Har-de-har-har. How've you been, Beth?"

"Andy and I are doing well, but the real question is, how is the elusive Ms. Harper?"

She could sense Selena's deep sigh even though she couldn't hear it. "I signed the papers today. Life as a full-time soldier is over."

Yes! "Great. When are you coming home?"

"Hopefully next Friday. I should have everything packed by Wednesday, so that gives me a day to relax, take a final drive around Oahu and say my goodbyes."

"Were you able to finish the training?"

"I did and I'll have to hand it to my CO. He really didn't believe I would stay, but knew those classes would benefit me whether I stayed in active service or the reserves."

"That was nice of him."

"Yeah. He told me I reminded him of his daughter. She's also in the nursing corps."

Beth retrieved the coconut flakes from the cupboard and sprinkled them on top of the cake. "Since you're coming back to the area, can I assume you'll be staying here at the bed and breakfast?"

"Yes, but only for a week or so."

Beth frowned. This was the part she'd been dreading—finding out where Selena would plant her roots. "Then where will you go?"

"It's a surprise. How's the house coming?"

Beth imagined the smile on her face could be seen from space, if anyone would be looking down. "You're not going to believe this."

Selena laughed. "I'm all agog. What now?"

"We're building on an addition."

"What? Wait, did the builder finish already? And you're adding on... oh my goodness. Beth Warren! Are you pregnant?"

Beth snickered. "No, we're a year or two away from starting a family."

"Then why would you be adding on?"

"Do you remember me talking about Grandma Belinda and Grandpa Paul?"

"Yes, Andy's grandparents. The Franklins, right?"

"Um-hmm, but they mean so much more to us. They practically raised Andy."

"Okay, so?"

"We're adding in-law quarters so they can live with us."

There was a long delay. "Why would you do that? You two finally get your own place, and now his grandparents move in with you?"

"They're the nicest people you'll ever meet. They came to visit last week. Grandma told us that some developer made a huge offer for their home in Ohio. And they've been talking about wanting to move closer to us and, you know... one thing led to another and, well, we decided to expand our home. It will be nice to have family living with us."

"Wow. Instant extended family, huh? Like the bed and breakfast, only permanent."

"Don't be such a Debbie Downer. You know I like having friends and family close. Speaking of which... where did you decide to plant roots?"

"I told you... it's a secret."

Beth took a final look at the cake before covering it. "Oh, I see how it goes. We're just BFFs, but if you want to be like that, fine. I'll change the subject for you. How's Reed?"

She was surprised by the change in Selena's tone. "That's something I need your help with."

***

The air was stifling inside the old house. Reed walked over to the thermostat, only to discover the device was set to heat, not cool. He'd been befuddled lately. Reed probably moved the switch when he adjusted the device before going to work this morning. After a few keystrokes, the fan kicked on. It would take a while before the interior of the house cooled down.

He changed out of his work clothes, grabbed a glass of tea and headed out to his patio. While the little yard would never win any awards, it was pretty. Growing up, he'd hated yardwork, but now found solace in gardening. After the last couple of weeks, he needed an outlet.

One of the frogs in his little pond croaked, trying to attract a mate. Reed started a conversation with his amphibian friend. "Hope you have better luck finding a girl than I did. But then, you're lucky being a frog. Me? Not so much. I'm the most despicable man God ever created."

The coolness of the glass he held was a sharp contrast to the early evening heat. "Maybe I should just move west and start over." He'd bungled up everything—his friendship with Trey, the closeness with Rose and the budding romance with Selena. "God, if You're listening, I really need your help down here."

His attention was drawn to one of the flowers close to where he sat. A large bumble bee flitted from bud to bud, collecting the pollen. It was a pink knockout rose. Like an idiot, he'd bought it in honor of his friend, hoping someday to show her his backyard paradise.

Taking another sip of tea, he forced the thought of Rose Sheppard from his mind. He searched for and found his froggy friend sitting on the lip of the little pond. "Just as well, you know. Since the day I met her, I knew I never had a chance. Her heart has always belonged to Trey." His mind then shifted to another girl, Selena, and the debacle of his downfall with her.

An irritating horse fly buzzed around Reed's head and landed on his cheek. It quickly took a bite before he could swat it away. He turned to the frog. "I'd appreciate if you could pick up the pace in keeping the fly population down."

In response, his amphibian buddy answered, *"Ribbit, ribbit."*

"I know. Here I am trying to control you, just like I tried to control Selena. No wonder she dumped me." He didn't understand why she had been so wishy-washy over leaving the service. They had spoken openly about seeing where things would go between them when she returned from Hawaii. That was before the Army offered her a different post. And like the fool he was, Reed only considered his own feelings. He had lost his temper with Selena, demanding she return here, where he was waiting. "The perfect incentive for any girl, right?"

A ping sounded on his phone. Picking it up, Reed discovered that it was from Trey. The day after the catastrophe at Longwood, Reed offered his resignation. Trey wouldn't accept it, but the two agreed to a change in his tasks. Reed would no longer be the service manager. Instead, he slid into the open plumber position. Both men agreed that it would be better if Reed spent as little time in the shop as possible, so Trey texted the next day's work tickets about this time every day.

He dropped the device back on the table next to his chair and then studied his hands. His fingers were trembling, probably because he hadn't eaten a bite since yesterday. Reed had no desire for food.

The things he craved were no longer within his reach.

Reed's mind wandered as he took in his lush backyard. *This place could be heaven, if only I had someone to share it with.*

The sound of a car engine echoed from out front, before the motor was turned off. Reed was in no mood for visitors. Though outside, he heard the doorbell ring several times before someone knocked loudly. *Just go away.* He didn't move, but instead anticipated the hum of the vehicle starting up. There was no such sound.

He had just taken another sip of his tea when he heard the latch on the garden gate squeak. From the corner of his eye, he caught the movement as the gateway swung open. *Maybe if I don't move, they won't know I'm here.*

He sat there in silence, not moving a muscle until he felt the touch of a hand on his shoulder. He shuddered as he faced the intruder.

Her smile astonished him. "Aren't you happy to see me?"

Chapter Fourteen

Reed continued to stare at the woman sitting across from him. They were in Sophie Miller's tearoom, with menus in front of them. Not where he thought he would be just a short half hour ago.

The lady's white teeth were a contrast to her deeply tanned face. She was still smiling at him. "I'm surprised at your greeting. I thought you might be more excited to see me."

"I'm waiting to wake up and find this is just a nice dream."

Selena laughed and then lightly pinched his arm. "Nope. This is real."

"But I thought we were through. I didn't even get a text back after I messed up."

The smile disappeared from her face as she studied her glass of iced tea. "We all make mistakes. I made one by leaving you hang. I was trying to decide if I was doing the right thing, career-wise, and didn't want any distractions. Despite being a nurse, sometimes I have issues multitasking."

"I was pretty sure you'd dumped me."

"That wasn't my intention. Can we have another try at this?"

She was even prettier than he remembered. "What do you have in mind?"

"Let's go back to where we were before I left. Is that possible?"

This was too good to be true. "Just like that, you could forget what transpired?"

There was something about her expression that sobered him. "Let me explain something. My mother died when I was very young. My father never complained about losing her. With the hand life dealt him, Dad could easily have been bitter. He could have turned his back on me because of his loss and the world wouldn't have thought much less of him. But instead, he put all his effort into loving me enough for both of them. Once, I asked him how he could do it, how he could live day by day without my mom by his side. Do you know what he said?"

"No, but please share with me."

Selena reached across and took his hand. "Dad said we all have a choice as to what memories we allow to play in our mind. He chose to remember all the great times he and Mom had shared. 'God blessed my life with your mother's love, if only for a brief while' was what he told me. Then he said, 'Remember, you have a choice on how you'll live. Will you allow happiness or bitterness to rule your life?'"

Selena stopped and waited until Reed was looking directly into her eyes. "We both have a choice in front of us. We can dwell on what happened and take our chances or we can decide to move forward. I think you are someone special. I don't wish to spend our time together quarreling. Can we put what happened between us in the past?"

"Is this real or have I gone insane?"

"What do you mean?"

"This is so unlike any other relationship I've ever been in. I mean, with every other girl, the first time I screwed up, I got dumped. And after what I did to you, you've got every right to toss me aside. But you're not doing that. Do I have this right? You want to just turn back time to before it happened. Is that correct?"

A smile slowly spread across her face. "That's what I'm proposing. What do you think?"

"That I'd be insanely stupid not to say yes. But are you really sure?"

"Of course." Selena offered her right hand. "Do we have a deal?"

It felt as if the weight of the world had come off his shoulders. "Yes, yes." Reed stood and opened his arms. Selena found her way into them.

They sat, but continued to hold hands. He was still in shock. "So, your days as a soldier are really over?"

"For the most part. I'm in the reserves now, and no longer on active duty."

"What does that mean?"

"Unless there's an emergency and the unit gets called up, my commitment is one weekend a month plus two weeks every year. And to answer your next question, I made a ten-year commitment. At that point, I can retire with twenty years of service."

Reed laughed. "What's this? Now you can read my mind?"

"Maybe." They halted their conversation when the waitress returned to collect their order.

After the girl gathered the menus and left, Reed turned to take in Selena's face. "Any guess about my next question?"

Selena dropped her chin into the palm of her hand and said, "Who's picking up the tab?"

That made him laugh. "No, that will be me. I was wondering if you'll be staying in Lancaster."

She looked away. "Not exactly."

Great. He finally met the girl of his dreams and she moves away. "Where then?"

Selena looked directly into his eyes. The piercing blue of hers was breathtaking. "Are you busy Saturday?"

"I am never too busy for you. Why?"

"I want to show you my new home."

"Is it close by or do I need flight reservations?"

"That depends on your point of view."

He couldn't help but stare at her in confusion. "You are such an unusual woman. What does that mean?"

"In the past, some of my friends have accused me of driving excessively fast. One, in fact, used to kid me about being a pilot, not a driver. He nicknamed my Charger the 'Millennium Falcon'. So, if you're up to it, I'll take care of the transportation. There's just one thing I ask."

"Which is?"

"Keep an open mind when we arrive at our destination."

***

Trey slid his vehicle to the curb in front of the Sheppard residence. While Rose had invited him to share supper with her family, he had a sneaking suspicion his girl's face might be the only friendly one at the table. He'd barely closed the car door when she appeared on the porch. Trey couldn't help but take in her essence as he approached. The blue flowered dress she wore accentuated not only her blonde hair, but made the blue in her eyes pop.

"Don't you look handsome tonight?"

His cheeks heated. "That would be a matter of opinion, I believe. But the way you look? I've never seen a more beautiful sight."

"Thank you." Rose took his hands and leaned her forehead in so as to touch his. They hadn't kissed since they made up, but this was Rose's way of greeting him intimately.

"Well, well. Look, everyone. The man returns to the scene of the crime. Hi, Trey."

He caught the blush on Rose's face as she glanced away. Trey had expected negativity from Lily. She didn't disappoint. "Evening, Lily."

"As requested, I set an extra plate for you. Do I need to get another place setting for anyone else? Like Selena Harper?"

Rose turned to face her sister. "Lily, please don't do this."

"After what he did to you?"

Trey knew he needed to be the one to address this with Rose's twin. "Lily, may I speak to you privately?"

He felt Rose's eyes on him. "What? You want to talk to her, by yourself? Are you crazy?"

"Maybe. If you can excuse us for a few minutes, I'd like to have a few words with your sister... alone."

"O-okay." Rose looked troubled as she stepped into the house.

Lily sat in the porch swing and pointed to the spot next to her. "You wanted to talk?"

After taking a deep breath, he engaged her eyes. "Look, I made a mistake."

"That was an understatement. You hurt my sister, badly. I can't stomach that."

"I didn't do it intentionally."

"Nevertheless, you damaged a loving soul. Now Rose tells me you made up with her. In other words, you've repented of your sins."

Lily obviously didn't believe him.

"She forgave me. Hopefully you will as well."

"Yeah, right. My sister has a pure heart and sees the good in everyone. I don't... because I'm a realist. You forget, I was there at the farewell party. I saw how you looked at Selena when she walked away from you."

"What do you think you saw?"

"Love. That's what was all over your face. You are still in love with that girl."

"I am not *in* love with Selena, but I won't deny that part of me still loves her. And, even though it is none of your business, as I explained to your sister, that love is in the past tense."

Lily shook her head and laughed. "And my naïve, older sister believed you, didn't she?"

"Rose did. But you don't, do you?"

"Nope."

"Okay. What will it take for me to convince you?" She had a funny little smile on her face. "Lily, I don't want to be at odds with you. Who knows where life may lead? There may be a day when we're related. And the last thing I want is for you to be at odds with Rose or me."

"You and me related? Really?" Lily held her hands against her cheeks to mock him.

Trey ignored her action. "Yeah, maybe... I don't know. So, all cards on the table. What's it going to take to convince you?"

Lily bit her lip as she studied him. Finally, she leaned forward and whispered in his ear, "I want to watch, firsthand. If you let me do that, I'll forgive you."

The girl was not only obstinate, but she was confusing. "What do you want to see?"

"I want to witness you telling Selena Harper that you are in love with Rose and that Selena means absolutely nothing to you."

"Now wouldn't that be rude?"

"Ah, so you're ashamed of Rose?"

"Absolutely not. I'm proud not only of her, but to be in love with her."

Lily opened her eyes wide and gave Trey a very large smile. "Then you shouldn't be afraid to let the world know."

"I am not embarrassed to tell anyone that."

"Good. How about telling Ms. Harper that she means nothing to you?"

"She knows that."

"Then it wouldn't be anything to say it in person, would it?"

If that would get you off my back... "To satisfy your curiosity, yes. But there's a problem with your gameplan."

"And that is?"

"The last I heard, Selena was in Hawaii. She didn't return like she said at the party, and I was told Selena had been offered another post if she stayed in the service. I think her next assignment is in Okinawa, as in Japan. Selena may never be returning to the area, ever."

The smile on Lily's face grew. "But if she would come back, you'd do what I asked?"

This is getting old. "Sure."

The girl offered her hand. "Let's shake on it."

He shook with her. "Great. Now do you mind if I get back to Rose?"

"No. Please do." Trey stopped in his tracks when she added, "I'll let you know when I have it set up."

She was, oh, such a pain in the you know where. "What are you talking about now?"

"A time for you to talk to Selena."

"Like I told you, she's somewhere in the Pacific."

"Hmm, if that's the case, she must have a doppelganger."

"Excuse me?"

Lily had such a wide smile. "You know—a twin. Either that or she's... back in town."

Trey was tired of this conversation. "Okay, I'll bite. Why would you say that?"

"When I was at the tea room for dinner the other night, your buddy Reed walked in with… guess who? Selena Harper."

Chapter Fifteen

Beth was chopping vegetables to put in the crock pot for supper. Selena sat at the bar, sipping her coffee. "Thanks for your suggestion, you know, about what to say to Reed. There was a lot we would have had to work through, if not for you."

Beth could feel the smile on her lips. "I can't take the credit for any of that. Andy's grandfather passed on that advice when we first got married. I can still picture Grandpa Paul at the wedding reception." Beth set down the knife and gripped her shirt as if she were grasping a pair of suspenders. She lowered her voice an octave when she imitated the man. "He stood in front of everyone and said, 'Now children'... That's what he calls us—as in *their* children."

Selena laughed. "I can't wait to meet these two. Go on."

"He says, 'In your time together, there will come a point when the two of you will disagree a little. Before you know it, your little quarrel has mushroomed into World War Three. And it will make you wonder if this relationship is really worth it. And that's where my advice comes in. At that point, both of you need to take a deep breath and look each other in the eye. Then, remember this day and what I'm about to say. Think about how much you love each other and realize that love is the most important thing you'll ever have in this life. And understand that sometimes, it's easier to wipe the slate clean and start over than to argue about fixing things, or even what the issues were in the first place.' Grandpa Paul was right. Andy and I have used that concept more than once. What we've found is that when we put each other first, the problem *always* goes away."

"Just like that?"

"So far."

"Wow, that advice was a real gem. Hey, I also wanted to thank you for reminding me what my dad had to say about my mom. That helped, more than you know."

"Your dad was a rock star, just like you. Are you and Reed doing better now?"

Beth smiled at the dreamy expression on her friend's face.

"We are. It's a shame I was too caught up with Trey in high school and didn't take the time to notice him sooner. Reed is not only cool, he's super funny."

"And not to mention *uber* attractive."

"That he is. By the way, I was wondering what you and Andy are doing on Saturday?"

"After I finish my chores, we're heading to the little farmette for a work day. We've actually come up with a name for our new home—Trail's End."

"That sounds just like the two of you. I love the name. How soon until you move?"

"That's still in the future, but the construction is under roof as of Monday. We tore down one of the old chicken coops, but might be able to salvage the other one. I can't wait to go buy some chicks. But for safety's sake, that tractor shed's gotta go. Andy wants to build a garage in its place."

"Sounds like the two of you have everything all planned out."

"Not really. We dreamed about this for so long, and now that it's here... I can't put it into words. This is the best thing to ever happen to me."

"I'm glad."

"Hey, just so you know, I invited my mom, Sam and the kids up in the evening. Andy suggested we could have a bonfire, toast hot dogs and make s'mores. It's the first meal we're hosting at our home. The plan is to eat at five. Would you care to join us?"

"Actually, I was going to ask if Reed and I could visit your place. What time might be convenient for us to drop by?"

"I think we'll leave here about nine-thirty. You can join us any time after that." Beth gave her a curious look. "Were you really already planning on coming?"

"Of course."

Beth noted the slight smile on Selena's face. "Can I ask why?"

"You know me. I like watching my best friend make her dreams come true." Selena drained her mug before placing it in the dishwasher. "It's been nice chatting, but I've got to get ready."

"What do you have going on today?"

Selena slowly turned so Beth could see her face. "I, Mrs. Warren, have a job interview as the manager for an emergency department."

Beth's mouth dropped open. "Really? Where?"

"At a hospital."

"Duh. I figured as much. Which one?"

Her friend giggled. "You never change, do you?"

Beth felt her face warm. Selena teased Beth about being a busy-body. "What are you saying? I simply asked you a question—you know, for your benefit. I was only trying to be polite and continue the conversation."

"Hah! Nice try, but the main reason was to satisfy your inquisitive mind by wanting to know *my* business."

"Well, there's no issue if your answer solves both purposes, right?"

Beth was surprised when Selena briefly hugged her. "Don't worry. I won't allow our friendship to fade away this time. Let's just say I'll now be close enough to visit but far enough not to get in your hair."

Making sure she stuck out her lip, Beth made her saddest face. "I would tell you."

"I know you would, but I don't want to count my chickens before they hatch. I promise I'll tell you, shortly."

"When?"

"How about Saturday?"

"Wow, you'll have an answer about the job that quickly?"

"Maybe, but there's another reason."

"What's happening Saturday?"

"We're coming to visit you, remember?"

"Oh, that's right. I forgot. Wait. Where did you say you were going today?"

Selena shook her head. "I didn't, but wish me luck. That was a nice try, though."

"All right, I'll settle for partial credit. In all seriousness, good luck. I hope everything works out just as you hope it will."

"Yeah. Me, too." Shooting a wink at Beth, Selena headed in the direction of her room.

***

Reed slid the cargo door open and extracted the hand truck from the cluttered interior of the work van. Wheeling the device to the rear of the van, he opened the double doors and slid the large box to the ground. After verifying he had the right model, Reed slit the bottom of the carton and lifted the cardboard covering away. The brand-new water heater shimmered under the hot summer sun.

Reed had just lifted the appliance onto the nose of the hand truck when another van pulled in beside him. Trey, his supervisor and former best friend, stepped out. Though they texted, the pair hadn't spoken or seen each other face to face since the day Reed offered his resignation.

Reed, not looking forward to even a brief discussion with his old friend, merely nodded. "Hi, boss. What's up?"

Trey pointed at the appliance. "Thought you might need a hand with that."

"Nah, I'm good. Thanks, anyway."

"Want some assistance taking out the old unit?"

"Nope. I can get it... all by myself."

Reed was about to pull back on the handles of the dolly when Trey touched his arm. "Okay, let me be direct. You and I need to talk... now."

After exhaling loudly, Reed sat in the rear of the van. "Go ahead, boss."

"Quit calling me that. This conversation isn't about work. What happened to our friendship?"

"Don't know what you mean."

"Come on. Since grade school, you've been my closest friend. Why has that changed?"

"Didn't know it had."

"Stop it, Reed. Tell me the truth."

"Okay, but remember—you asked for it." He paused, wondering if his words would forever end their friendship. He looked Trey directly in the eye. "I'm tired of watching you always get the best of everything."

"Are you talking about the business? I offered for you to go in business with me in the very beginning, but that wasn't what you wanted. And a couple of years ago, I gave you a chance to be a full partner in the company, based only on the sweat equity you'd already put in."

"I'm not talking about your business. You were the one who thought up and built this endeavor from the bottom up. I wouldn't want to take any of the credit from you."

"Then it's about women, isn't it? That was the real reason you offered your resignation. You were jealous Rose and I got everything worked out, weren't you?"

Reed felt his fists clinch. "It wasn't only about Rose Sheppard."

"Now you're bringing Selena into this as well?"

"You weren't happy when I questioned if you would mind if I asked Selena out. I've known you since, like forever. You wanted *both* women."

"How would you feel if I asked out someone *you* used to love?"

"That's beside the point."

Trey studied him for a moment before continuing. "Really? That question might not be as far off the mark as you're pretending."

"Which means?"

"Rose hasn't put it together, but I do believe I have."

"What are you talking about?"

"You're in love with Rose and have been for a while."

Reed felt like he'd been drenched with a bucket of ice water. "Why would you say such a crazy thing?"

"Hmm. Ladies and gentlemen, the witness avoided directly answering the question. I will give you credit, Reed. At least you didn't deny it."

"Again, what are you trying to get at?"

Trey shook his head. "You seem to know everything about Rose. I took notice of how much you knew about her when she and I finally got around to dating. And then, when we had the argument, Rose cleaned out her desk. The note she left was clearly addressed to me, but you opened it anyway. In all the years we've known each other, that's the last thing I would have expected from you."

Reed felt trapped, as if there would be no positive outcome from this conversation. "Enough. I'll just quit now and get out of your life. I never should have intruded in your personal world like that."

"But you did and, to your credit, you knew exactly where Rose could be found."

"That was a mistake, me going there."

"Rose told me that a couple of times you referred to yourself as 'her best friend' that day, did you not?"

"Look, I'll finish this job and turn the keys in this afternoon."

"I was oblivious to all of it… until you suddenly quit. After all these years and the issues we've worked through, why would you do that?"

"I didn't want to be around and watch you two argue again. That's why."

Trey touched him on the shoulder. "Is that the real reason you stepped down from the Service Manager's position… or was it so you wouldn't have to face Rose anymore after you realized the way you felt about her wasn't mutual?"

Reed shook his head, but didn't answer. If he spoke, he might break down. Trey placed a hand on both shoulders.

"It's okay. I understand it all now. You love Rose, and believe me, I understand why. Rose is the perfect woman. Yet before I went out with her, I asked if there was something between you two. You denied it, several times. Why couldn't you tell me the truth?"

Jumping to his feet, Reed shoved his friend away. "Because I never had a chance with her. Rose has been in love with you since the day she started. Since I couldn't win her heart, I tried to be a friend—her best friend. And then, when you two split..." His voice trailed away.

"You thought she would finally notice you—and understand how much you loved her all along."

This was the end, a bitter, humiliating defeat. His feelings were naked before Trey. "Yes. You hit the nail on the head." Searching in his pocket for the van keys, he said, "Now you know the whole truth. I was in love with your girl. I'll admit it, I tried to pick her up on the rebound. Aren't you happy you're so smart?" He yanked the fob from his pocket and shoved it into Trey's hands. "Here, I quit."

Trey backed away and didn't take the keys. "Stop it. We've been friends for most of my life. I don't want to see our friendship end. We'll work this out." Trey studied him. "But I need to ask one thing first. Something else played into what happened that day, didn't it?"

The numbness filling his mind and body overwhelmed all of his defenses. "Yes."

"What was it?"

"Selena Harper."

Chapter Sixteen

Selena pointed the rental car west after driving through the traffic circle in Gettysburg. Glancing across the seat, Reed was looking out the window, taking in the sights. She stopped while a string of pedestrians trotted over the crosswalk at the next intersection.

The man shook his head. "There's an awful lot of tourists in town today. I don't see how people living in Gettysburg put up with it. I know I couldn't."

"Oh, I'm sure the locals have learned to adapt. They probably use the roads that are less traveled and modify their schedules to avoid the congestion."

"I don't know about that, Selly. I camp up here for a week every summer and let me tell you, the number of tourists just seems to grow year after year. Almost exponentially."

"You camp here? I didn't know that. Why?"

"I always liked history. When I was a teenager, one of my aunts researched our family tree and discovered two of my long-lost uncles fought with the 88th Pennsylvania Infantry Regiment at Gettysburg. I've retraced their steps and have hiked every corner of the battlefield."

"How come you never shared that with me?"

"It just never came up."

"That's interesting. I wonder what else you might have kept from me."

"In time you'll hear it all, probably to the point of nausea."

"I doubt that. Maybe you'd be willing to share your knowledge of the battlefield with me someday?"

He smiled at her. "It would be my honor."

Time to find out more about Reed. "Do you like this area?"

When she glanced across the seat, he shrugged. "I guess it's okay. I'm kind of partial to eastern Lancaster County."

"Don't all the Pennsylvania Dutch tourists bother you?"

Reed laughed. "I guess it's like you said earlier, us locals learned to adapt and stay out of their way. But I am curious. Why did Beth and her husband buy a place up here in the middle of nowhere?"

"They're planning on starting a family... sooner than later. Both of them expressed to me they want to raise their kids in an environment that's slower—and less complicated than where they currently live. One of the first things I noted when I returned to Lancaster was how urbanized the area has become. And while I love Lancaster, I'd much rather be in a rural environment."

"Not every inch of Lancaster County is built-up."

"True, but to go shopping or travel to work, one will have to put up with all that congestion."

"You do have a point. Speaking of work, how did your interview go?"

She was suddenly giddy, thinking about the situation. "They made me an offer that I'm giving serious consideration."

"Congratulations! Which hospital? The Lancaster area has so many of them to choose from."

They were driving past an airstrip just north of town. "It's not in Lancaster County."

"Okay. Where is it? York, Dauphin or Berks? Maybe even Chester County?"

"How do you feel about Cumberland County?"

Selena could feel his eyes boring into her. "That's not close at all to Lancaster, unless you're talking the southeastern part of the county. Is the job near Harrisburg?"

"Not really. It's a little farther west."

"Why would you consider a job way up there?"

"Because this is where I decided I want to plant my roots."

***

"Slowly, that's it. Now take up the slack." Andy had attached a heavy cable to Beth's Explorer. The other end was wrapped around one of the beams of the dilapidated tractor shed. When all the slack was gone from the hawser and the old wooden building shifted a little, she stopped.

Andy climbed in the vehicle beside her. "Are you ready?"

Beth shook her head and giggled. "I can't believe I'm actually doing this."

He also laughed. "You'll love it. How many other girls can say they demolished a building?"

"Okay, I'm ready. What should I do?"

"Back up, but gradually. You only want to make it collapse, not spread debris over the entire state."

Her hands trembled as she gripped the steering wheel. "I'm a little scared."

Andy leaned over and kissed her cheek. "It will be fine. I'm right here beside you... and always will be. Okay, whenever you're ready."

Easing her foot off the brake, Beth gently touched the accelerator. A creaking noise filled the air as the structure moved along with her, as if they were dancing. The old walls slowly returned to a vertical position before shifting in the direction of her SUV. All of a sudden, the entire building quivered and then fell, threatening to cover Beth's car. She gunned the motor and pieces of splintered wood flew everywhere.

"Honey, stop!" Immediately following her husband's instructions, they waited in silence as the dust cloud slowly dissipated. "Put the transmission in forward and ease up a little. Great, hold it right there. Drop it in park and let's check out what you did."

They exited and Andy disconnected the cable. Beth felt as if she'd won the lottery. "I can't believe you let me do this. That was fun!" Clapping her hands, she jumped up and down. "Can we do it again?" She pointed at the old chicken coop they had shored up previously. "Let's pull that one down, too. We can always build another."

Andy laughed. "You're a goof ball."

For the next two hours, they carried timbers and chunks of broken lumber, making a pile of it in the clearing Andy had wrested from the vegetation.

Beth and Andy had just sat down on lawn chairs to take a break when the low crunch of tires on stone filtered through the trees that hid the driveway.

Selena's rental car peeked through the foliage along the drive. Her friend's arm shot out of the window in salutation. Beth and Andy waved in return and waited while Reed and Selena walked over to greet them.

Beth pointed to a stack of folding chairs and a cooler. "Get something to drink and have a seat."

The expression on her friend's face was one of mirth. Beth knew what was coming next—teasing. "We drive all this way to see what you've done and what do we find? The two of you drinking iced tea and relaxing. You could have done that in Lancaster."

Before either of the married couple could respond, Reed piped in. "Something's missing. Is it my imagination or didn't there used to be a building there?"

"How observant," Andy answered. "We tore down an old coop over there." He pointed at a bare area. "And you just missed it. My wife, the human bulldozer, just razed the tractor shed." Andy motioned at the pile of debris waiting to be burned. "That's all that remains of it."

Selena whistled. "Always knew Beth was good for something. At least now we know what it is."

"Selena Harper! I thought we were friends."

"Oh, we are. That pile will make a great bonfire to roast hot dogs."

Andy shook his head. "They're calling for rain in the morning. We'll burn it then."

Selena turned to Beth's husband. "Why wait? Everything's lush and green, so the risk of a forest fire is low, right?"

Beth caught the smile Andy offered her. "Mom and my siblings are coming up. We don't want to take a chance on one of them getting burned. And as Andy pointed out, that wood is probably coated with lead paint, so we can't cook over it. My husband, the planner, brought along some seasoned hickory for tonight's fire."

The unmarried pair both nodded. Selena's eyes drifted to the structure that would one day be their home. "Do we get a tour or must we wait until it's finished?"

Beth's chest swelled with pride. "Now is as good of a time as any."

Andy extricated himself from his chair and helped Beth from hers. Hand in hand, they strolled to the partially constructed house. The exterior walls were made from concrete block. The foursome stepped around the scaffolds to enter the Warrens' future residence.

Inside, Beth curtsied as she faced the pair. "Welcome to Trail's End. You have just entered what will be the mud room." She stepped a few feet deeper inside. Pointing to her left, she continued. "Off to the left will be the laundry. To the immediate right will be the full-sized pantry. Farther down and in front will be the children's play room… eventually."

Stepping to the left wall, she held her arms as if revealing a surprise. "This will be where the stairs are located." For the next half hour, Beth acted as the hostess, describing the location of not only the rooms in their side of the home, but also the function and location of the in-law quarters in the yet unconstructed addition. Despite never leaving the ground level, Beth explained the layout of each floor. Occasionally glancing at Andy, her heart filled with delight, because their dreams were finally being realized.

After the tour was over, they again sat and refreshed themselves with tea. Several minutes of laughter passed before Selena whispered to Beth, "I need to use the restroom."

Beth felt her eyes widen when Selena got to her feet and started to dance around. She pointed to a porta-potty. "There's one there for the construction guys."

Selena gave her a strange look. "You expect me to use that, after they did?"

"Well, it's either that or drive a couple miles to the convenience store."

"I'm not sure I can wait that long."

Beth had a hard time holding her chuckle inside. "Then there's always nature. Plenty of trees around. You should be used to that kind of thing... I mean since you were in the Army and stuff."

Selena shot her a dirty look. "I was assigned to hospitals and places that had real latrines. Come on. Hop in the car and navigate for me."

After a quick conversation with Andy, the two women jumped into Selena's rental and headed out of the lane. At the end of the drive, Selena pointed to the vacant house across the street. A sold banner hung across the For Sale sign.

Selena turned to Beth. "Do you know if anyone moved in yet?"

"I don't think so. Why?"

"I bet it has a bathroom."

"I'd hope so, but I'm sure it's locked."

Selena shook her head. "Lock, schmock. I'm in a hurry and drastic times call for drastic actions."

Selena whipped the vehicle into the drive of the vacant building. As soon as the car was parked, Selena flung open the door and ran around the corner of the building.

Beth checked the surroundings to make sure they were alone before following her friend. Her mouth almost dropped to the ground when she saw Selena standing in the threshold of the open door.

"Selena Harper! What are you doing? That's private property."

"Hurry up and be quiet. Let's get inside before someone notices us."

Beth pushed the door shut and followed Selena up the stairs. "So help me, if we get arrested, I will never forgive you."

"Waah, waah, waah. Just enjoy our escapade. Go to the front room and keep an eye out to make sure no one is coming."

Beth snuck in the empty room and peered through the curtain. "The coast is clear, but hurry up. You're lucky. I'm surprised they didn't turn off the water."

Still keeping an eye for movement outside, Beth almost jumped out of her skin when Selena tapped her shoulder. "What do you think of the color of this room? Are the mint green walls and forest green trim too much?"

"What? Are you nuts? Let's get out of here. I can only guess how badly this is going to end up if the owner arrives and wants to know who I am. You might get away with it, but I'm their neighbor. I can only hope they don't press charges."

Selena apparently thought the whole ordeal was funny. "Come on. Where's your sense of adventure? While we're here, let's look around." Her friend's voice floated from down the hallway. "This room would make a nice nursery, don't you think?"

"I can't believe this. Have you lost your mind?"

"Why? Because I want to check out the place? Just like you would normally do. Wasn't it just this week you were trying to figure out what I was doing, because you're nosey?"

"That was different."

"No, it wasn't."

Just then, Beth heard the sound of a car on the paved road outside. She dropped to her knees. Selena peered through the curtains as if she owned the joint. To Beth, it appeared that the sound of the vehicle changed. "Did that car stop?"

Selena nodded as she gazed at Beth. "I'm afraid it did. You are busted."

"Great, the owner of this house is probably here."

Her friend shrugged. "Maybe, let me go downstairs and check." Beth almost fainted when Selena left the room and trotted down the stairs. "Hello? Oh, hi there. Come on up. Who am I? Oh, that's not important, but I would like to introduce you to your new neighbor. Her name is Bethany Warren and she lives down the lane across the road."

Under her breath, Beth muttered, "So help me, Selena…"

There were footsteps on the stairs. "Beth? Come out and meet your new lady neighbor."

Beth hesitated, wishing she would wake up and find this was but a dream.

"You'll have to forgive my friend. This is her first felony and, to be honest, the entire thing was her idea. You know, she doesn't think she looks good in orange, but I'd disagree."

Selena! You just threw me under the bus! Beth wished she were anywhere else but where she was.

"Beth, are you coming out to meet your neighbor or not? I know you're in that bedroom, hiding. You have to understand that she does this all the time. What? Oh, I didn't mean break into houses, I meant the whole being nosey thing. You need to be careful. She might just bug your house."

Beth's face was on fire and her hands were soaked with sweat. "Okay. I'm coming." As she opened the door, Beth apologized, "I'm so sorry we have to meet under these circumstances. It's just…" She stopped mid-sentence when she found Selena standing at the top of the stairs, all alone.

"Where is she?"

"Who?"

"My new neighbor."

Selena shrugged and then smiled. "You're looking at her."

Beth shook her head in confusion. "What? I don't understand. Weren't you talking to someone?"

Her friend shot her that one-sided smile she kept in her pocket for when she pulled off a joke. "Just like I told you. Close enough to visit but far enough not to get in your hair."

"This is confusing. Who was in the car?"

"Oh, that was your parents. They headed back the lane to your place." When Beth didn't answer, Selena smiled. "Howdy, neighbor."

Chapter Seventeen

Reed walked into the shop and sat in his old chair at the service desk. It felt strange after spending so much time on the road, working as a plumber. It was hard to believe Trey had talked him into resuming his old role.

Stacked around the desk in a large pile of clutter were the supplies that had been delivered while he was 'on assignment', as Trey told everyone. A stack of paperwork loomed in the inbox. It would take days to straighten out this mess.

Rolling up his sleeves, Reed grabbed the first box and headed to the stock room. He had just unloaded the parts from box number seven when he felt eyes on him. As much as he wanted to shrink to the size of an ant and crawl away, he knew she'd be waiting. Reed raised his head to meet the woman's gaze.

Rose Sheppard sat in his elevated swivel chair. Her smile greeted him as she offered him a mug of coffee. "Welcome back, stranger. Brought this for you."

Reed's tongue clung to the roof of his mouth. *How much did Trey tell her?* Reed managed a nod.

Rose diverted her gaze so she was looking at the floor. "I want to say this, so please don't stop me." The girl drew a deep breath before continuing. "I think you are the least selfish man I've ever met."

He recoiled. That certainly wasn't what he expected her to say.

The beautiful blonde continued. "You filled in as a plumber because we were short. Trey said he told you that wasn't necessary, but you did it anyway." She stopped to sip from her mug. "And when Trey and I had our blowup, you sensed it. I apologize for being angry at you for reading the note, but I'm glad you did."

"I shouldn't have—"

The lady raised her hand for him to be quiet.

"I am so amazed that you knew where to find me. Even though I didn't admit it then, I will now. You being there that morning, well, it meant the world to me."

Reed was speechless. Though he knew it would never be, he would've given anything in that moment to hold her.

"You said something else that touched me—that you were my best friend. I thought about that long and hard. And you know what?"

She paused and met his eyes. The words sounded foreign coming from his mouth. "What's that?"

Rose touched the back of his hand. "My mind went back to the first time we met and every day since. I've never had a truer friend than you. So selfless and genuine. You're a shining example of how God tells us a friend should be. And I thank the Lord for bringing you into my life."

It was torture not to pull Rose into his embrace and find her lips. But she wasn't his and never would be. "I'm the one who is blessed to have you as a friend."

"Thank you. Can you do me a favor?"

"I'll try."

"Promise me that you'll never quit being my friend, okay?"

Reed stuck out his hand. "Deal."

Much to his surprise, the beauty wrapped him in a tight hug and whispered in his ear, "Thank you for being you."

It was the hardest thing he'd ever done in his entire life, but he allowed her to pull out of his embrace.

Rose's smile was like morning sunshine after a long, dark night. "Lily told me she saw you and Selena at dinner a while back. Is she finally back from Hawaii?"

"Yes. Selly decided to leave the service. She's staying at Ellie Campbell's B&B, for right now."

The girl lowered her voice, even though no one else was around. "Are you two dating?"

"Kind of, for now."

"What do you mean, for now?"

"Selena is moving to upper Adams County. She took a job in Carlisle."

He could not only see, but felt Rose's compassion as the color drained from her face. "How's that going to impact your relationship?"

"I'm not sure. We'll have to see what happens."

"That lady is a remarkable woman. She deserves a good life partner. Someone strong and vibrant, well-mannered, thoughtful." She paused, waiting to continue only after Reed met her gaze. "She needs someone like... like you." Her face was suddenly pink. Rose nodded at the cup she'd given him earlier. "Enjoy your coffee, and Reed, welcome back. I missed you."

Without a further word, she headed for the office. Words slipped from his mouth. They were comments not meant for anyone else to hear—ever. "Why couldn't she be you?"

***

It didn't happen overnight, but the old place Selena purchased was slowly becoming a home. Reed stopped up one or two nights a week and usually on Saturday afternoons. He was a good friend, because there was always something that had to be done, and he always volunteered to assist. Sure, Reed often stayed for dinner or the pair managed to sneak in a quick walk, but the majority of Selena's life involved work. If it wasn't managing the ED at the hospital, it was painting or cleaning or making out bills or washing clothes or something involving being a responsible homeowner.

The bright spot in Selena's life was her relationship with Beth. They had never been closer. As soon as Beth's little sister, Missi, returned from school, the younger woman took over the position managing the B&B for the Campbells. And when the two siblings felt comfortable Missi had everything in hand, Beth and Andy moved in with Selena. It would only be temporary, of course, because the builders were getting close to finishing the Warren house.

All three adults were busy in their own way. While Selena worked at the hospital, Beth prepared meals and cleaned Selena's house before heading over to work on her own place. Andy left early in the morning, then spent his evenings doing stuff at the farmette. But the friendship between the two women had become stronger than ever.

One Friday evening while on the way home from work, Selena received a call from a number she didn't immediately recognize. Without a second thought, she answered it. "Hello?"

"Hi, Selena. It's Lily Sheppard. Remember me?"

"Of course. How have you been?"

"I'm well. Someone told me you're working for a hospital in Carlisle."

"Um-hmm. I manage the ED for the hospital."

A moment of silence. "I'm not sure I heard you correctly. You manage what?"

"The Emergency Department."

Lily snickered. "I guess I watch too many late-night television commercials. How do you like your new job?"

"I love it. I'm not so sure all my employees appreciate having a former Army officer for a boss, but things are coming along nicely. How are you and your family doing?"

"We're all doing great. I actually have a boyfriend now. I'm not sure if you remember Nate, one of the cute guys who helped with Youth Fellowship?"

Selena didn't, but wasn't about to be rude. "Kind of. Didn't he have dark hair?"

"Yep, that's him. The cute guy with glasses."

It had been a stab in the dark, but hey... even a blind squirrel finds a nut from time to time. "Oh yes, Nate. Such a nice guy. Well, good for you."

"Thanks. I understand you've bought a house north of Gettysburg."

"I did. It's quite peaceful up here."

"Is it anywhere close to Caledonia State Park?"

Why would Lily want to know that? "It's just down the road. Why do you ask?"

"Later this month, Rose and I are taking the youth group up there for the day. We were going to have a picnic and maybe spend some time in the pool. I know the kids would love to see you. It will be a very low-key day—just my sister and me chaperoning the kids. Would you like to join us?"

While the thought of bantering with Lily wasn't very appealing, Selena had enjoyed chatting with the kids in youth fellowship. It had also been a while since she'd seen Rose. "Let me think about it. If I do come, may I bring Beth Warren?"

"Absolutely. The kids liked her as well. Just shoot me a text so I know how much food to bring. Nice chatting with you."

After getting home, Selena showered and walked next door to look for Beth. She found her friend in the barn, applying stain to the trim the carpenters would soon install. The odor was quite pungent. "Good grief, what in the world is that smell?"

Beth set down her brush and walked outside with Selena. The girl removed her gloves and a respirator. "Sorry. That's the stain. It uses aliphatic hydrocarbons as the carrier for the tint component."

Selena laughed. "Ali-what? Oh, that's right. I forgot you married a safety nerd."

"Hey! Why would you call my Andy a nerd?"

"Duh, he has you wearing gloves and using a respirator."

Beth lifted her chin for effect. "That's because he loves me and doesn't want me to get cancer from over-exposure to toxic chemicals."

"I've never seen anyone else wear a respirator when staining wood."

Beth had a grin on her face. "If they ever read the safety data sheet they would. How was your day?"

"Boring. I spent the whole day working on next year's capital budget. I'm beginning to hate spreadsheets. You?"

Beth was wiping the sweat from her face with a disposable cloth. "I painted the ceilings on the second floor. I would have started on the walls, but the electricians arrived and started doing electrical stuff."

"How much longer are you planning on working this evening?"

"Actually, I was only waiting on you to drop over before I quit. Let me clean up and then we can walk back to your house."

While Beth tidied up, Selena inspected Beth's new home. The stone masons had finished the exterior. In several places, the craftsmen had inserted rich, red bricks that gave the appearance of being used to fill a hole in the stone surface. Beth and Andy had selected windows with dark brown grids in them, so that, along with the darkly stained beams that bordered the stucco facing, they gave the house an old-world Tudor appearance.

Beth appeared. "Hey girl, I'm ready. Anything exciting in your world?"

"Not really. Oh, I forgot to tell you. Lily called me on the way home."

"Lily Sheppard? What did *she* want?"

"She called to invite us to a picnic. She and Rose are bringing the youth fellowship up to Caledonia and want us to join them."

"Us?"

"Yeah, you and me. I told her we come as a package deal these days."

"Really? To what do we owe this great honor?"

Selena offered a frown. "Why are you such a pessimist?"

"I'm not a Lily fan. Rose is fine, but something about Lily bothers me. Why'd she pick us?"

"She said the kids liked us, but I'm not sure that's the case."

"What? Why wouldn't they like us? I mean, we're the two coolest women in the galaxy."

"I didn't mean that, you goof ball. I think they're low on chaperones. Probably worried about the kids carrying on in the pool."

Beth stopped and swung Selena toward her. "Have you ever been in the pool at Caledonia?"

"No, why do you ask?"

"The pool is spring-fed and it's freezing. That's where they send ice cubes to cool down."

Selena laughed. "You should be glad Andy married you because there's something definitely wrong with you. He's the only one crazy enough to put up with you."

Beth's expression sobered. "Is Trey going to be there as a chaperone?"

"Lily said it was just her and her sister. Don't you want to come?"

"Somehow, I'm not sure Lily told you the whole truth. Something's suspicious. I'd better come along to protect you."

They turned and continued walking to Selena's house. "Just don't make me wear gloves and a respirator."

Chapter Eighteen

Rose squeezed the hand of the gentleman standing next to her. The church service had just finished. Her heart fluttered with anticipation of an afternoon spent together. Just before reaching Trey's car, Lily appeared.

"Can I bum a ride home with you guys?"

Rose turned to Trey, who simply shrugged. "That's fine with us. Didn't you come with your mom and dad this morning?"

"Yes, but they decided to go out to lunch with some friends. They're all heading to Buca Di Beppo in Reading."

Trey had an expression of confusion on his face. "Never heard of it. What type of cuisine do they serve?"

"Italian, but they serve it up family style. You order from the menu and then share with your party. Haven't you ever been there?"

"No, I haven't." He glanced across the seat to Rose. "Do you like their food?"

Rose couldn't help but smile. Since she and Trey started dating, it felt like she was finally living the life God had planned for her. "I love everything they make. Perhaps we can go there sometime, if you'd like."

"Maybe I can invite Nate and the four of us can go out. Would that be all right?"

"Sure, why not?" Trey answered.

Rose's eyes drifted to Trey's face. Despite his response, she could tell he wasn't thrilled at the prospect. Ever since Trey had come to dinner after they reunited and Lily confronted him, something was off between them. When Rose questioned her sister later, Lily stated she had simply expressed to Trey her displeasure at him hurting Rose. Rose was certain something else had transpired, but she'd allowed it to slide.

After returning to Leola, Rose changed into a bright sundress and cute sandals, but packed a set of walking shoes. She grabbed the picnic basket she'd prepared earlier. Trey had used the guest room and had changed into shorts and a tank top Rose had given him.

Back in the car, she tuned the satellite radio to '70's music. It was a beautiful day. "I can't believe how quickly summer is passing. Only two weeks until Labor Day."

There was a special glow in the man's face today. "I know. Hey, I was thinking... have you ever been to the beach?"

"Only once and that was when I was a little kid."

"Which beach did you visit?"

"It was down south. My parents took us to Disney World, and then we stopped at Myrtle Beach on the way back."

"Did you enjoy it?"

Rose reached for his hand, tracing the outline of his fingers with her own. "It was fun, I guess. Unfortunately, I never learned to swim. Why do you ask?"

Trey's eyes had that funny kind of excited look about them. "Would you like to go to Rehoboth Beach for a long weekend?"

"J-just the two of us?"

"Yes. A friend of mine has a beach house. I usually rent it for a week or two in the summer, but this year was kind of crazy. You know, since I met this beautiful woman, she's had a monopoly on my time."

A chill ran across her shoulders. "Is that a good or a bad thing?"

His wink answered before he could respond. "It was the best thing to ever happen to me. Getting back to my offer, I was hoping we could drive down Wednesday evening and return on Labor Day. What do you think?"

"Would it only be you and me?"

"I was hoping so. I mean, I haven't invited anyone else."

Rose hesitated. Even though she was an adult, she could picture her parents' outburst about going away with Trey for a weekend, by herself. "I'd feel better if we could invite at least one other couple."

He eyed her strangely. "After all this time, are you concerned about the two of us being alone? I mean, I've tried to treat you with respect and dignity. Even if we would share a room, that wouldn't change."

"I know, but others might not understand."

"As in, your parents still don't like me?"

"It's not that, but could we bring others?"

His sigh was sad. "Who would you like me to invite?"

"Maybe Lily and her boyfriend?"

"If that's what you want, then yes."

"Thank you. Can I ask one more favor?"

A smile slowly spread across his face. "Absolutely. Ask and it's yours."

"Could we invite Reed and Selena as well?"

He nodded.

"May I be the one to invite them?"

His face darkened. "Sure."

***

Selena smiled as Beth placed a container in Selena's new car, a Subaru Crosstrek. "This is a really nice car, though I think the color is a bit much."

She couldn't resist the urge to tease her friend. "You don't like orange? I specifically picked this one out because I think you look great in that color."

"You know my favorite color is blue."

"But orange accentuates your beauty. Just think, a jumpsuit in this shade would make the color in your eyes pop."

"And here I thought you were my friend. You're teasing me because of the day when I thought we broke into that house—which I later discovered was *your* house."

"Well, it was your idea... you little jailbird."

"I think all those x-rays your patients have had are beginning to affect your mind. You quit wearing those lead aprons, didn't you?"

"So not true. What's in the basket?"

"My mom sent along some whoopie pies for us to share with the kids."

"But Lily said not to bring anything. The girl said she made all the food herself."

Beth snickered. "Have you ever had any of Lily's cooking?"

"Well, no. What are you insinuating? Have *you*?"

"No, but I just wanted to have something really good on hand in case. A girl can never be too careful."

Selena was thankful for the day off from working at both her real job and around the house. "Then I'll just say thanks for watching out for me. Are you glad I moved in next to you?"

"Of course. Now I can keep a close eye on you. Do you think Trey will be there today?"

She shrugged. "It makes no difference to me. He belongs to Rose and I'm glad for them."

After a moment of silence, Beth spoke up. "How are things going between you and Reed?"

Selena knew she was frowning. "He's not happy I moved up here. Reed is a good friend, but I don't believe he thinks of me as anything more than a friend... since the move."

Selena kept her eyes on the road, but felt Beth's gaze boring into her. "Is there a question behind that stare?"

"Kind of. I thought the two of you had something special going on, or did I misread it?"

"I wouldn't mind, but I detect his heart is focused elsewhere."

"Did you bring it up to him?"

Selena lifted the turn signal for the park entrance. "I've met a lot of men since high school. None of them was the right one. I want to be wanted... for me. You know, I'm jealous of you. You and Andy have this fairytale romance thing happening between you. And that's exactly what I want. I hope you know how rare that is."

"Does that mean Reed isn't your Prince Charming?"

"If he is, I must have driven past the sign. Maybe it's because we've both been so busy. Perhaps we simply need a little time alone." She slid the car into a space between two minivans. At a pavilion not very far away, the faces of the twin Sheppard sisters sported smiles as they waved.

Selena returned the gesture, but then grabbed Beth's arm. "Certain things I've shared between us are just for you and I, okay?"

Her friend squeezed her hand. "Yes. Best friends forever. I would never betray you... even if you did try to get me arrested."

Before they could get to the roofed building, the youth surrounded both women. One teenage boy plucked the basket from Beth's hands. When they got to the table, Rose hugged both of them. Lily followed suit and Selena believed the girl's action was genuine.

Lunch was already spread out on the table and after Rose offered the prayer, they all enjoyed the feast. Selena watched Beth's reaction as her friend sampled the macaroni salad and then the pulled pork. She had to suppress a giggle when Beth asked for seconds. Her friend didn't even seem to be upset when Lily told the youth they could eat the snacks Beth brought only after dipping in the pool.

The late summer sun may have been hot, but the waters of Caledonia certainly didn't fail to cool everyone down. The four women briefly joined the youth in the frigid water, but quickly retreated to the pool chairs.

"Thank you both for coming today," Rose said. "This is a lot of fun."

"Yes," Lily added. "We should do this again sometime... soon."

Selena caught the look the sisters shared. Some unspoken communication was going on.

Rose opened a can of diet soda and looked at the two friends. "Do either of you have plans for the holiday next week?"

Selena shook her head, but Beth piped up. "Andy and I are traveling to Ohio to visit Grandpa Paul and Grandma Belinda."

Selena turned to her. "I thought you'd be spending it with your family."

"No. Mom and Sam have farmer's markets next Friday and Saturday. Then they're going to the big party at the Campbells' on Sunday."

Rose again asked, "What about you, Selly? Do you have plans?"

"Well, apparently I don't... now."

Beth touched her arm. "I'm sorry. You can certainly tag along with us. Andy's grandparents won't mind."

"That's generous of you to suggest that I invite myself to Andy's grandparents' house, but I'll pass."

Rose had an excited look on her face. "Then maybe you could join us. We're going to the beach."

Lily nodded. "It will be a lot of fun. Trey invited Nate and I to join them."

"And you and Reed are also invited," added Rose. "The beach house where we're staying has plenty of space. I was hoping we could have a clambake right on the beach. It's going to be a great time. Please come."

"We want you to come," Lily chimed in.

Selena glanced at Beth from the corner of her eye. Her friend smiled and shrugged. Beth silently mouthed, "You wanted some time alone with Reed."

Lily spoke next and Selena wondered if she'd read Beth's lips. "Even though we'll all be together, that doesn't mean we'll spend every second as a group."

"I don't know."

Rose smiled. "Please? You're my friend and I really want you to go to the beach with us."

Selena wondered if she would regret her answer. "Okay. Let me ask Reed first."

Rose shook her head. "No need. I already asked him and he promised he'd come, but only if you wanted to."

"Then I guess it's settled."

Lily had never smiled as widely. "I can't wait."

Chapter Nineteen

Trey opened the door to the beach house. "Here we are." The other three adults followed him inside.

He could tell Rose was nervous when she asked, "Where are our rooms?"

Pointing up the stairs, Trey answered, "There are five bedrooms upstairs and four in the basement. I was thinking the ladies could take the second floor and the guys could stay on the bottom floor. I mean, after all, there is an air hockey table down there, so the men can scarf that up."

He had joked with Rose all week about having to share rooms. Now that she knew he'd only been kidding, her voice was relaxed. "Do you mind giving us the grand tour?"

The house was spacious, containing not only a large eat-in kitchen, but a formal dining room. The *piece-de-resistance* of the first floor was the gigantic gathering room that overlooked the ocean, complete with a stone fireplace. After all the supplies were lugged in and properly stowed, Trey grabbed a bottle of water. Stepping outside, he found an Adirondack chair on the porch. From his vantage point, he could easily watch the waves roll ashore.

He sensed Rose's presence before she came into view. The light touch of her hand on his arm sent pleasant sensations across his whole body. "It's even more breathtaking than I remembered."

His girl sat next to him, holding his hand. In the distance, a freighter plowed up the Delaware Bay, bound for Philadelphia. Seagulls called each other names as they searched the sand for anything edible. A little higher in the air above them, a small plane plodded along, towing an advertisement for one of the local restaurants.

He thought he detected a longing in Rose's eyes, perhaps a desire to explore the shore. Trey picked up on it. "Do you want to take a walk along the beach?"

She nodded, but her gaze didn't waver from the water. Hand-in-hand, Trey led Rose to the edge of the surf. He laughed when she jumped as a wave exhausted itself on the sand right at her feet. The fresh breeze, carrying with it a slight salty tang, ruffled her long blonde hair.

As they strolled, Rose entwined her arm through his. They had walked about half a mile when she stopped and slowly turned him to face her.

"The beach is even more beautiful than I remember."

"It's my favorite place. I'm glad you enjoy it as well."

Standing on her tiptoes, Rose gently rested her forehead against his. "This moment is even better than my memories, because you are here." Moving her head away, she searched his eyes.

The next words she spoke took him off guard. "I love you, Trey."

Even more surprising, for the first time since their breakup, her lips found his. The taste of Rose's lips and the warmth of her embrace carried his thoughts away. A wave broke just before them, splashing water up to their knees.

His mind wandered and it was as if he was out of his body. He could see himself standing on the beach, holding the woman of his dreams in his arms. The face of the woman slowly materialized before him. In shock, he jerked away, blinking rapidly.

Rose still held him. "Are you okay?"

"Yes, yes. I thought I felt something sting me."

"Was it a bee or maybe a jellyfish?"

"I don't know. Let's head back to the porch and get some dinner, okay?"

"Sure. I'd follow you anywhere."

Her head was on his shoulder as they returned to the cottage. He knew he should be thinking of Rose, but he couldn't get the other woman's image out of his thoughts. The one of the girl he'd been kissing in his mind—Selena Harper.

***

The shadows were getting long. Selena hadn't been able to get away from the hospital as early as she'd hoped, plus traffic on this holiday weekend was horrendous. By the time she reached Reed's house, it was pushing seven. He was waiting on the porch, bags next to his chair.

Selena had barely turned off the engine when he met her at the car. "Sorry I'm late."

"Don't mention it." His words didn't match his apparent mood. In less than a minute, he'd loaded his gear in the trunk. He hopped in and tugged his seatbelt across his body. "It doesn't look like you packed much."

Looking over her shoulder so she could back onto the road, Selena shrugged. "The Army taught me to pack only what was necessary for the mission. Thanks for going to the store and picking up what we were supposed to bring. I'll settle up with you later."

"That's fine. Did you eat yet?"

"No. I was in a hurry to get here, but traffic was a bear."

He huffed. "I thought you were going to leave by three. That would have put you here at four-fifteen or four-thirty at the very latest. We could have been in Rehoboth by now. What delayed you?"

"There were staffing issues and then the hospital administrator called me into her office. We had an urgent issue we had to discuss."

"A text would have been nice."

She looked at him with growing agitation. "I did text you. Did you look at your phone?"

Reed shifted position so he could dig the device out of his pocket. "You did not send any such text. Here, I'll prove it to you."

"Really? Let's review the tape."

An eerie stillness filled the vehicle. "Well, excuse me. I stand corrected. There are three, no, make that four texts you sent. Unfortunately, my phone didn't alert me."

"Did you have it silenced?"

"Do you think I'm stupid? I most certainly..." Reed threw the device on the floor. "I did."

"So now what? Are you going to be upset with me only for tonight or make it an all-weekend long project? If that's the case, let's turn around now and save both of us from the agony."

The breeze from his sigh could have extinguished a hundred candles. "Selly, I'm sorry. I was just looking forward to this weekend so much and I guess, I guess I overreacted. Can you forgive me?"

"Yes. I'm sorry it took so long. We're going to have to come to an understanding about my job."

"What do you mean?"

"As a manager, I can't just leave when the clock says it's quitting time. If I'm in the middle of something, I need to finish it."

"Is this the way it's always going to be?"

Selena nodded. Reed just didn't get it. "Yes. Unfortunately, that's the way the health care system works."

"What if you were a plain nurse instead of a manager?"

"Reed, it wouldn't matter if I was a nurse's aide or the hospital administrator. We have a duty to care for our patients." He was staring out the window. "What would happen if someone had a broken pipe, but it was quitting time? Would you put away your tools and say goodnight?"

"Now that's different. People need water. And if I had something going on, Trey would cover."

"Thanks for enlightening me. Human beings need their water, huh? News bulletin—they need health care as well." Her expectations for the weekend were deflating by the minute. "Why don't we just drop it? I'll apologize for being late and we'll let it be."

"I want to ask one other question before we stop."

He can't leave well enough alone. "Go ahead. Fire away."

He pivoted to face her. "Why did you have to move so far away?"

"We discussed this before. It's where I chose to live."

"Yeah, well I'm not happy about it. You didn't even ask me."

Selena was so angry that she was having a hard time concentrating on the road. "I didn't know I needed your permission to decide where I was going to live."

No more comments came from that side of the Subaru for several miles. His voice was softer when he finally did speak up. "Can this be one of those times where we just forget the argument?"

"But we didn't resolve anything."

"I beg to differ. I learned a lesson."

"Which was?"

"Our argument happened because, once again, I allowed my feelings to take control. I should have thought of you first. I'll try not to let it happen again. Deal?"

It was her turn to drop a deep sigh. "Sure. I think we need to stop for supper. That might help things. It could be we're both hangry. Any suggestions?"

"There's a bunch of fast-food places in Wilmington. That would be the quickest choice, then we can get on with the trip. Is that all right by you?"

"Sure, on one condition."

"Which is?"

"Let's try to enjoy the trip as much as the destination."

Chapter Twenty

The sun hadn't yet risen. Trey carried the little beach chair to the edge of the water. The Atlantic had been warmed from three months of summer sun, but Trey couldn't tell it this morning. The cold saltwater lapping at his feet chilled him to the bone. It was about six-thirty and as far as he knew, Trey was the only one awake.

About fifty yards off shore, he watched a pod of dolphins work their way north, parallel to where the waves wet the sand. Trey had turned in early last evening. He was drowsy, but not yet asleep when he heard commotion from upstairs—Selena and Reed had arrived. Trey's eyes were still open when the other two men turned in, almost three hours later.

A lone seagull flew overhead, his *ha-ha-ha-ha* call accompanied by the roar of the endless waves crashing ashore. Trey's mind drifted back to the previous evening. But it hadn't been the noise or the laughter that kept him awake. Instead, it was the vision he'd had as he held Rose in his arms. Why had his mind replaced Rose's gorgeous visage with Selena's deeply tanned features? While each woman was beautiful in her own way, he knew he should be concentrating on that long blonde hair which framed a perfect face and endless blue eyes. She was the future God intended for him, wasn't she?

An exceptionally large wave caught him by surprise and drenched his whole body, almost knocking him out of the chair. He shook his head. Did God send that wave to slap him in the face like a wake-up call to redirect his attention at Rose? Or was it an admonishment for breaking a pure heart ten years ago?

Closing his eyes, he was suddenly back in Selena's arms, at the time right after school ended, before he stupidly destroyed both of their futures. There had been no doubt Selena loved him. She had endured his pain and cheered his few triumphs as if they were her own. True love like that was surely a blessing from God.

"Selena, if I could go back in time, I would..." He stopped. It was too late. Those days were long gone, forever. He couldn't fix it... couldn't change the outcome. Some mistakes were eternal, and this was one he'd regret until his dying day. In frustration, he covered his eyes with his hands.

A slapping noise to his right jarred him back to reality. Those were the sounds of a jogger's feet on the wet sand. Quickly wiping the moisture from his face, he turned. His mouth was suddenly dry as he realized who was sharing the early morning hour with him. The woman slowed and offered a warm smile.

"Morning, Trey."

"Hi, Selena."

They stared at each other. Her face was indeed thinner, but Selena was even prettier than he remembered. He struggled to find something to say.

She beat him to it. "Such a pretty morning. Did you come out to watch the sunrise?"

The best he could manage was, "Um-hmm."

She walked until she stood behind him. "I see the rays in the distance."

Trey turned to observe the horizon. "It won't be long now."

A few seconds passed before she continued, words barely a whisper. "Do you remember how sometimes we'd get a notion and drive all the way down here, just to watch the sunrise?"

Those memories were followed by many others the pair had shared when they were young and in love. Selena's left hand touched his left shoulder. Without thinking, he reached for it and their fingers intertwined. Simultaneously, they squeezed each other's hand tightly.

Across the water, a golden haze slowly rose above the surface. A few seconds later, the rim of the earth's only star breached the horizon. His memory again traveled back in time. Silently, he lipped the words that the two of them had made up as their special morning beach prayer.

"Thank you, God, for a new day. Let this be a day of peace and love. Help us celebrate this new morning You created—just for us. Please bless our time together and make the memory of this day one we'll cherish forever. Amen."

Whether it was his imagination, or a trick of the wind or maybe Selena's actual voice, Trey wasn't sure. But he knew for a fact he'd heard the words as clear as day. "...one we'll cherish forever. Amen."

Selena released his fingers and much to his surprise, pressed her lips gently against his hair. He knew the next words truly were spoken by the girl he once loved as she whispered in his ear, "Thanks for those memories and for sharing today's sunrise with me."

He suddenly was overcome by the need to hold her. But it was as if his body was momentarily paralyzed. By the time he'd willed himself to stand, Selena had continued with her jog and was perhaps a hundred or more yards distant.

Trey shook his head. Did he just imagine what happened? Selena's figure grew smaller as she ran northward. That's when he felt it. Someone was watching him. Glancing at the beach house, he discovered exactly who it was. The woman standing at the rail didn't look happy. Lily shook her head, then turned and walked inside.

***

After a jog that lasted almost two hours, Selena stepped into the dwelling. The enticing aroma of bacon filled the air. She was heading up the stairs when Rose stuck her head out of the kitchen.

"Morning, Selly. Trey said you were out for a run. Did you have a good time?"

For the most part, she had. "It was exhilarating. Maybe you should come with me tomorrow."

The blonde's smile was heartwarming. "I might just do that. Breakfast is almost ready. I'm making scrambled eggs and bacon. Come join us when you are ready. We'll wait for you."

"Thanks. I'll be down soon."

She grabbed her clothes and headed to the shower. She hadn't meant for her run to last as long as it did. But that brief moment of watching the sunrise with Trey had ripped opened a vault of memories. Ones she had locked away forever, or so she'd thought. But this morning, they spilled from her memory into her heart, messy, like when she once dropped a three-pound bag of elbow macaroni on the floor. To force the remembrances from her active memory, she'd continued her morning ritual. Now, things inside her heart were back to normal. For the most part.

Her hair was still wet when she stepped onto the porch. The other five were sitting around one of the tables. Rose laughed as Selena approached. "There you are. We were just talking about you."

She surveyed the group. Reed smiled at her, but Trey quickly looked away. Lily's face revealed no expression. A chill scampered across her shoulders. "Really? What were you saying? Good things, I hope."

Reed pulled out her chair and then pushed it in after she sat. "I was saying how glad I was that you came with me."

Trey still didn't glance at her when he muttered, "Nice brownie points."

To Selena's surprise, Lily suggested, "Maybe you should take notes."

"Shush. Trey is a perfect gentleman." Rose's voice appeared to have a calming effect on her sister.

"I was mentioning about how brave you are, to have refocused your life after the service. Even though I wish you lived closer, I'm happy you bought a home near your friend Beth. Maybe someday you'll invite us to see it."

"I think we could do that, though it's nothing like this place."

Amusement was evident in Reed's eyes. "What she means is—not yet, but with the to-do list she keeps for me, it will soon eclipse the beauty of this meager shack."

Selena turned to face him, barely hiding her smile. "Really? Wait until you see your task assignments next time you visit."

Trey cleared his throat. "Now that we're all... *finally*... here, can we eat? I'm starved."

To Selena's surprise, Lily offered a beautiful prayer. Not only did she praise God for the splendor of the day, she asked Him to refresh their souls. The last portion of the prayer struck a deep chord within Selena. "And Lord, we each find ourselves standing at a crossroad today. Help us select the right path, the one You would choose for us. Amen."

The serving dishes were passed around and Selena noted that Rose had added red peppers, black olives, mushrooms, onions and cheese to the eggs. The food was scrumptious. And while she hated to admit it, Selena was just a tad envious of Rose. Not only did the beautiful woman have a kind and friendly heart, she apparently could outcook Selena any day.

After breakfast, the group split. While the men went golfing, the three women shopped. Much to

Selena's surprise, without the men around, Lily was exceptionally nice to her. Later, all six of them met for dinner at an elegant restaurant and then returned to the beach house. The sun was bidding them farewell when she and Reed took a stroll along the surf. They didn't talk a lot, but with their arms entwined, words weren't all that necessary. Perhaps they were rebuilding the closeness that had faded.

They turned around to return to the house in the deepening evening hues. Up ahead, she could see the other four adults frolicking in the waves. When they were maybe thirty yards from the group, Trey started jumping up and down in the waist-deep waves. His voice had an urgency to it when he called out, "Rose, where are you? Rose! Rose!"

There was no answer. Less than five seconds passed before Lily started screaming for her sister, but again, no response. Reed freed his arm and ran into the waves, close to Trey.

Selena was perhaps two steps behind. "What happened?"

Trey's words were high-pitched. "She was right next to me a minute ago."

"She can't swim," cried Lily. "We've got to find my sister!"

The men turned and stared at the water.

Selena took charge. "Trey, move ten yards to your left and begin your search. Nate, ten yards on the other side of Trey. Reed, take the area where you are. I've got the far right."

The four of them began searching beneath the waves, but the growing darkness dampened their efforts. Just as she'd been trained, Selena dove beneath the waves, swimming side to side as she hunted for Rose. Prayers for her friend filled her heart. After each cycle, she broke the surface and tried to peer across the waves. Nothing. Time was their enemy. With every passing second, the probability Rose would be found alive diminished.

Selena breached the surface, now perhaps fifty yards off the beach. Reed's scream rent the stillness of the night air. "I found her! Help, help!"

Turning toward the noise, she could make out his shape another thirty yards farther in the bay. With swift, strong strokes, Selena headed his way.

When she reached him, Reed was doing his best to keep his head above the water. He held Rose's limp body in his arms. He was sobbing.

Selena grabbed his arm. "Give her to me."

"She's too heavy. I'll keep her here while—"

"No!" Selena screamed. "We need to get her onto the beach. I'm the strongest swimmer. Let me take her."

When Reed didn't respond, Selena threaded her arm around Rose's chest. Doing her best to keep Rose's head above the water, Selena kicked and clawed her way through the Atlantic surf.

After what felt like an eternity, Trey and Nate were there, standing in the chest-deep water. The pair carried Rose's limp body to the dry beach.

Lily was beside herself as she knelt in the sand next to her sister. The younger twin's voice was almost hysterical. "She's not breathing. Please God, don't take my sister! Help, help! Someone, please help!"

Despite near exhaustion from the swim, Selena forced her way to Rose's side. Shoving both men out of the way, she felt for a pulse—none. She grasped and turned Rose's body on its side as she cleared the airway. Water drained from the girl's mouth. Selena shouted, "Trey, call 911!"

Selena then turned the woman onto her back. Pinching Rose's nose shut and lifting her chin, Selena gave four hard rescue breaths.

Still nothing.

Feeling for Rose's sternum, Selena interlocked her fingers and began chest compressions with increasing force. Suddenly, Rose's body shuddered and the blonde began coughing violently.

Selena again turned Rose onto her side. "Nate. Quick, get something to cover her with. I don't want Rose going into shock."

Reed knelt next to her. "Is she going to make it? Please, don't let her die. I need Rose."

She had to push him out of the way. "Move. Give Rose some space."

Rose coughed and gagged while she continued to spew water from her lungs. Lily was sobbing loudly. The younger twin wrapped her arms around Rose in an effort to keep her sister warm while waiting for the blanket.

Selena swept Rose's hair to the side. "How are you doing?"

The woman's eyes were wide. In between coughs, Rose managed to get out, "I'm okay."

By the time the police and ambulance arrived, Rose had been carried to the porch and was swaddled in blankets. After checking her out, the paramedics transported Rose to the hospital. Lily rode beside her in the ambulance, while the other four followed in Trey's car. Shortly after midnight, Rose was released.

Back at the beach house, Nate built a roaring blaze in the fireplace. Rose sat on the couch, with Lily on one side and Trey on the other. All attention was focused on her.

Rose seemed to be in a trance, but after a while, she said, "Thanks to each of you for helping me. I didn't think I was going to make it."

Lily hugged her sister tightly. "But God brought you through."

Rose nodded, then turned to stare at Selena strangely. "There's a purpose for each and every thing that happens. Tonight, I guess I discovered why God brought you into my life, Selly. At the hospital, they told me I'm alive... only because of what you did. Thank you." Rose struggled to her feet and approached Selena. Her rescuer stood and the two embraced. Rose whispered quietly in her ear, "My soul tells me tonight was only the first reason God brought us together."

Selena pushed Rose away so she could see her face. "What do you mean?"

"I'm not sure, but somehow, I feel our futures are dependent on each other." The golden-haired woman shrugged before turning to the group. "Good night, everyone."

Rose struggled up the stairs, accompanied by her sister. Selena felt eyes on her. Slowly, she turned to find Trey staring at her intensely. He nodded then disappeared down the stairs.

Her thoughts went back to Rose's words. *Our futures... dependent on one another?* What did that mean?

Chapter Twenty-one

After the drama from the night before, everyone slept late. The weather had changed and a steady rain waited for them outside. Trey felt that was just as well, because Rose told him she wanted to spend the day resting on the porch. Lily and Selena made breakfast, allowing him to spend time with his girl.

But something was different about her. Rose was pre-occupied. A couple of times, he had to repeat himself before she responded.

After the meal, Rose curled up on a wicker loveseat and fell asleep. He covered her and walked inside to where the other two women were doing dishes.

Lily glared at Trey, then glanced at Selena before looking away.

Selena's question almost startled him. "How is she?"

"Rose?"

Selena shot him a look as if to say, "Who else would I be talking about, dummy?"

He recovered. "She's tired."

Lily pulled up a stool and perched herself at the bar. "My sister was awake most of the night. I think she was scared to go to sleep. Maybe it was caused by the memory of the trauma or possibly because she was afraid she wouldn't wake up if she did fall asleep."

Selena poured all three of them a cup of coffee. Without asking, Trey noted she prepared his drink just the way she used to. "What exactly happened last evening?"

Closing his eyes, Trey's mind replayed those terrible moments. "I was introducing her to the ocean. We were out in the water where it was up to her neck. I was teaching Rose how to use her toes to bounce and float on the waves. All of a sudden, we lost touch of each other. When I turned, she wasn't in sight. I quickly searched for her under the water, but couldn't find her."

Nodding, Selena asked, "Did anyone warn you about rip currents in the area?"

"Not this time. Maybe last year someone might have said something, but I don't remember. It shouldn't have been an issue because I was right there with her. Last evening was all my fault."

"Yes, it was, but thank God Selena was there." He pivoted to find Lily staring at him. "Whether you agree with Rose that everything happens for a reason or me—that we are given a choice—there's no doubt God brought Selena here to spare my sister's life."

Trey ignored the twin and gazed at Selena. "How did you know what to do?"

"Do you mean setting up a search grid to find her?"

"Yeah, that too. But I mean, that had to be an almost super-human effort just to get her on the beach. Not to mention saving her life. How could you put it all together so fast? Are you some super-hero in disguise?"

Selena studied her cup. "Trey, a lot has gone on in my life since you knew me. I've been trained to help people when they're at their worst. The Army drilled me over and over again on how to save lives. I'm not the silly high school girl you remember. What you saw is me, the woman I've become."

"But, you were like—"

Selena touched his arm to quiet him. "Don't dwell on this. I did nothing different than any other nurse would have done in the same situation."

Trey was aware Lily was turning her head to focus on whichever one was speaking, as if she were watching a tennis tournament.

When Rose's sister again spoke, he wasn't surprised. "Thank you again, Selly, for saving my sister's life. We both owe you." Then she turned to face him. "Don't you have something to say to Selena?"

Looking directly into Lily's eyes, he was confused. Lily had a sad smile on her face. There was further confusion when she shook her head before walking out of the kitchen. She called over her shoulder, "I'm going outside to check on Rose. Catch you both later."

It was now just the two of them. His palms were sweaty. "Th-thank you."

Selena drained her mug and then patted his hand. "You're welcome."

"I still can't get over the fact that you saved Rose's life."

"It was a life worth saving. You found a real gem in that girl." Selena's eyes were welling up. "You messed up ten years ago, so let me tell you something. You better treat that lady right, because if you don't, I'll punch you smack in the nose. The United States Army drilled me on how to do that as well."

Selena quickly left the kitchen. Trey noted his whole body was shaking, but he wasn't sure why. Was it because of what happened last night with Rose or what had just happened with Selena? And he didn't even understand what had just occurred.

He finally found the courage to join the others outside. When Trey arrived on the porch, he saw Lily and Selena standing at the railing, conversing as they scanned the sea. Nate was in a chair at the far end of the deck, reading a book. But he was most surprised to find Reed, seated not more than three feet away from Rose as she slept, watching her with bleary eyes and moisture on his cheeks.

***

Trey wasn't the only one who noticed Reed's interest in Rose. Selena did as well. The man she'd driven down to the beach with had also fallen silent. In the late afternoon, the rain moved out, leaving behind light breezes and patchy clouds. Nate and Trey started a nice bonfire. With Lily and Selena's help, they steamed clams, crabs, corn and potatoes. Reed remained on the porch, hovering over Rose.

After the meal, to Selena's surprise, Rose faced her. "Will you take a walk with me?"

The other four also stood, but Rose added, "Just the two of us."

"Sure." Barefoot, they strolled in the packed sand. When they were out of earshot of the group, Selena asked, "What's on your mind?"

It was a while before Rose answered. "First, I need to thank you for saving my life."

"I'm just glad I was there."

"Me, too." They walked a little further in silence before Rose continued. "Do you remember the day we met?"

"Yes."

"At our introduction, I felt as if I already knew you, like we were old friends."

They stopped and waited for a wave to recede from the beach.

Selena replied. "I felt the same."

Rose continued. "There appears to be some kind of connection between us. This may sound strange, so please hear me out. Yesterday, when I lost my balance and got pulled out to sea by the current, I had a vision."

Selena shivered in the evening air. "Would you like to tell me more about it?"

The lady nodded and wiped her cheeks. "I believed my life would be saved... and I fully knew it would be by you."

"Your mind might have been projecting that because of the trauma."

Rose shook her head. "Maybe, but I don't think so."

"Why do you say that?"

"Because there was more to the vision, a whole lot more."

"I don't understand."

The blonde drew a deep breath before continuing. "I think my life flashed before my eyes. The vision started in the here and now, with you saving my life." The chattering of a passing gull drew their attention. "But the dream progressed throughout the years. You were at my wedding and I celebrated at yours. We held each other's babies. Our families visited frequently and we took wonderful vacations together. I saw us comforting each other when loved ones passed on." The other lady stopped. Rose's gaze was fixed on something in the distance.

After a moment, she continued. "You were there, right next to my husband, holding my hand when I drew my last breath... when the Lord called me home. And I was there waiting, the first soul to greet you when you reached Heaven." Rose was scanning the horizon when she next spoke. "Somehow, I felt as if our futures were intertwined, almost as if we were closer than sisters could ever be."

Selena's nose was wet. "It sounds like a beautiful dream."

"It was, but there was more, so much more."

Rose had turned to face her. Something about Rose's expression was unsettling. "Please continue."

"A huge obstacle came between us. It all but ruined our friendship. I think maybe it was a warning from God."

"What do you think He was saying?"

"It was quite plain. That if we really wish our lives to be as He revealed in my dream, we'll have to trust in Him and acknowledge this friendship is one He ordained. For whatever reason, I believe it is His will for us to be close. But to follow the path He desires, no matter what comes, we need to trust His word and hold onto each other."

The expression on Rose's face had changed. It was sober and pure. Selena felt as if the woman was revealing her innermost thoughts. Rose suddenly looked directly in Selena's eyes and again spoke, "Do you think I'm crazy?"

The lady had just gone through a near death experience. As a nurse, Selena knew first hand of others who had had wild dreams when they were on the brink of life or death. "No, of course not."

Rose's hands began to tremble. "Well, that might be about to change. Maybe we should both sit down. I need to tell you about the rest of my vision."

Chapter Twenty-two

Selena knocked on the door. From somewhere inside the house, she heard Beth call out, "Come in."

The home the Warrens shared always had a homey scent. Closing her eyes, the image of apple pie laced with brown sugar and cinnamon filled her senses. Selena's mouth watered as she sat at the bar and waited.

"Want a cup of afternoon tea?" Beth entered the kitchen wearing a blue shirt with the image of Rosie the Riveter and the slogan "We Can Do It" below the figure.

"There's nothing I'd love better than tea and some adult conversation."

"Black, green or herbal?"

"Something with chamomile, if you have it."

"Done." Beth removed a box from the cupboard and then placed a teabag in the Keurig. By the time their tea had brewed, Beth slipped a generous slice of fresh apple pie a la mode in front of Selena. "How was Rehoboth?"

"It was the strangest experience of my life."

"Really? In what way?"

"Well, to begin with... Rose almost died."

"What?" Beth had to cover her mouth to keep from spitting out her food.

After the initial shock, Selena described in detail how the incident had transpired.

"Wow! She was lucky you were there."

"Maybe, but she thinks my presence was more than pure chance."

"How so?"

"She believes God put me there to save her." After Selena described the conversation with Rose about the dream, Beth brewed them each another cup of tea. Selena offered a weak smile. "Kind of weird, huh?"

"Not really. I believe God does interact with people all the time."

"But her vision? Don't you think maybe it was her mind exaggerating the situation?"

"It could be, or maybe it was something else. When my stepdad Sam almost died in the fire, his dead sister Jenna was there to save him."

Selena remembered that horrible time, when a family enemy had set fire to Beth's house and almost killed Beth and her stepdad. But Beth had never mentioned a dead aunt. "Stop making fun of me."

Beth set down her cup and waited until Selena was looking at her eyes. "I'm not. I saw his sister there in the burning house, too. Right beside him when he rescued me. As sure as you're sitting here with me. Sam almost gave his life to save mine that night, but Jenna was there—his guardian angel—to rescue him. And Jenna told Sam that God sent her

... not only to help him live, but to remind Sam that his purpose in life wasn't over."

"How does this pertain to what Rose saw?"

Beth stirred her tea. "I believe God speaks to each of us in different ways. Sam and Jenna were close. I think God delivered his message to Sam through his sister. For Rose, maybe because of the closeness she has with the Lord, He spoke directly to her through the vision."

Selena pondered Beth's words. "Did I tell you this part?" She shared the remaining contents of Rose's dream. After she finished, Beth's face was pale.

"Do you think she made it up?"

Slowly shaking her head, Selena answered, "Reed has always been close with Rose. The way he acted when the outcome wasn't for sure gave me an indication of the depth of their friendship. But when I found him watching Rose as she slept on the porch... I knew. Hearing her tell me about the dream confirmed my suspicions."

"What about the other part of her vision?"

Selena shrugged. "Only time will tell."

***

Reed was struggling. He knew Selena suspected his deep affection for Rose. He never was good at hiding his feelings. His mother used to tell him he wore his heart on his sleeve. But seeing the woman he cared about so much almost die in front of him... and knowing there hadn't been a thing he could have done to save or protect her... It was almost too much.

A knock sounded on his door. Walking to it, he swallowed hard. Selena stood outside holding a paper sack. "Hi, stranger. Can I come in?"

"Sure. This is a surprise."

"I brought us a meal. I take it you haven't eaten yet, have you?"

She'd always been able to read him. It was that "your heart is like an open book" thing his mom kidded him about. "No, I didn't. Let me grab a couple of plates."

"Hope you're in the mood for Chinese. I ordered beef lo mein for you. That is your favorite, if I recall correctly?"

"Um-hmm. You know me well."

"That, I do. All too well." He detected a tinge of sadness in her words.

The pair ate in silence. After finishing her spring roll, Selena asked, "How's Rose?"

"Okay, I guess. Haven't seen much of her this week."

"Why's that?"

"Oh, I've been as busy as a one-armed paper hanger. We're still a plumber short, so I spent a lot of time on the road. Besides, Rose missed a number of days of work."

Selena grew quiet, but her gaze made him uncomfortable. He tried to redirect the conversation away from his work... and Rose. "How was your week?"

"Challenging, and chaotic. There was quite a bit of adversity caused by one of my senior managers. He's a real pain in the neck, but I handled him. Like my daddy used to say, 'What doesn't kill you makes you stronger'. You ever feel like that?"

More than you'll ever know. "Occasionally."

"But I've found the best thing to do is to face your problems—a direct assault. First, come up with a plan and then slay the dragon. Do you agree?" Selena's eyes fell on him as she paused, waiting for a reaction.

It was suddenly very cold in the room. "Are you talking about work... or something else?"

She didn't answer immediately. He noticed Selena was pushing her food around her plate instead of eating. The woman didn't look up. "Reed, I want you to be happy in this life."

This was turning into a difficult conversation. The last thing he wanted to do was talk about feelings. "I am happy."

"Really? What's the greatest joy in your life?"

"Work, I guess. Why are you asking?"

Her laughter took him by surprise. "I was testing you, and your answer confirmed my suspicions."

"What do you mean?"

"What you said tells me there's only one of two possibilities."

"I am not following this conversation."

"It's simple, Reed. I know you well enough to recognize you didn't tell me the truth. So, either you told me a fib or you are lying to both of us."

"Why would you say that?"

Her smile was melancholy. "It's okay. You can be honest with me."

The food he had eaten felt like a lump of lead in his stomach. "I am."

"Really? Let's find out. Will you answer just one simple question for me? And swear on a stack of Bibles that you're telling me the truth."

"Y-yes, of course."

"How long have you been in love with Rose Sheppard?"

***

Rose sat alone in her parents' gazebo. The sun was approaching the horizon, but it was still very warm. She was studying the ladybug that had landed on her palm instead of deciding what to do. *Was it just a dream or a vision from God?* Rose was so deep in thought that she didn't hear Lily approach.

"Rose?" She snapped her head to attention and found her twin sitting next to her. "I'm worried about you. I don't think you've said ten words to me since we left Rehoboth."

"Sorry. I've been weighing a few things over in my mind."

"Did I do something wrong?"

Rose noticed her sister's eyes were puffy, as if she'd been crying. "Of course, you didn't." Rose gently pushed the ladybug to a nearby plant and then reached for Lily. The two sisters held each other for a long while.

"I know I haven't always been the best sister to you, Rose."

"Shh, you're fine."

Lily smoothed Rose's hair. "I'm scared. What's going on with you?"

"Nothing, really. Don't worry about it."

"That's not possible. We share more than blood. Please talk to me."

Taking a deep breath, Rose spoke. "Okay. When I went under the water, I had a vision."

"About what?"

Rose hesitated. "Let's just say it was about the direction God has for my life."

Lily nodded. "And you're struggling with it, aren't you?"

"Yes."

"Well, whatever it is, I'm here, right beside you. If you need someone to talk to, pick me."

As Rose looked at her sister, a lifetime of memories flashed by. "Thank you, but this is one path I have to travel on my own. I think this is the hardest thing I've ever done."

"You don't have to do anything alone. Not while you have me by your side."

Before Rose could answer, Mrs. Sheppard called out, "Rose, you have a visitor."

Rose looked at where her mother stood. She suddenly felt lightheaded. Lily turned to Rose before glancing in the direction of the house. Lily covered her mouth with her hands. "Oh, my goodness. The look on your face... This has something to do with Trey, doesn't it?"

Rose mumbled, "Yes."

"He's here. Do you want me to stay or go?"

"Can you give us a few minutes alone?"

Lily nodded, but then firmly hugged her sister. "I love you. I'll be just inside the door if you need me."

"Thanks. Love you, too."

After Lily departed, Trey walked over and sat down, facing her. "Hey there. You called off sick again today. How are you feeling?"

This was going to be harder than she thought. Tonight would be the night she broke it to him. "Not very well."

Trey's face was full of compassion. "You haven't been yourself in a while. It's been three weeks since it happened. Perhaps we need to have a doctor take a closer look at you. You might have a concussion or something."

She shook her head. "It's not my body that's the problem."

"Perhaps it's post-traumatic stress. There are professionals who can help you with that, too."

"I don't think that's the issue, either."

Trey waited a moment before continuing. "I only care about what will make you whole and get you feeling better. I love you, Rose. How can I help?"

She swallowed hard. *Here goes.* "I love you as well, but I don't think you and I-I-I sh-should see each other a-a-anymore... I mean besides at work. And, if that's not okay with you, I can quit. Not immediately. I'll stick around long enough to train my replacement unless you want me to leave right away."

He jumped to his feet. "What? You want to break up? Where did this come from?"

"Look, I made a mistake, Trey. When I saw you for the first time, I, uh... it was just..."

"Wait. This has something to do with Lily, doesn't it?" He turned in the direction of the house and yelled, "Lily! Come out here, right now."

Rose was confused. "What are you doing?"

He again called her twin before facing Rose. "We'll get to the bottom of this, right this instant."

He had no sooner spoken when Lily and both of her parents ran into the gazebo.

Lily was out of breath. "What happened?"

Trey pointed his finger at Lily's face. "You, that's what. What did you tell your sister about Selena and me?"

Rose was utterly confused. "What do you mean? You and Selena? Did something happen?"

He shook his head as he glared at Lily. "You couldn't leave well enough alone, could you? You saw what you *thought* happened on the beach and couldn't wait to use that against me, could you? Ever so anxious to drive a wedge between us."

Lily's face was white. "Trey, I didn't say a word to her or anyone. And oh yes, I saw what happened. But when Rose nearly drowned, I thought she'd suffered enough, so I kept my mouth shut."

The veins in Trey's temples were protruding. "I don't believe you."

Rose stepped between them and placed a hand on their arms. "Whatever happened doesn't matter and," she faced Trey, "Lily didn't say anything to me about you and Selena." Everyone there was breathing hard. Rose continued. "Don't blame my sister. You want to know what the issue is? When I almost died, I had a vision."

Trey took a step back. "You had a what?"

"God spoke to me, Trey. He revealed that I'm not supposed to be with you. And I'm not the woman He intended for you to love."

"Really? What, do you have a direct conduit to God? If it's not me, then who does He want you to be with?" Trey's face reddened. "No, no, no. Don't even tell me. It's Reed, isn't it?"

Rose shook her head. "Reed had nothing to do with my vision. Could you please calm down?"

"Then if it's not him, it must have something to do with that long walk you and Selena took, doesn't it?"

"Look, Trey..."

The man's eyes were wild. "I see the writing on the wall. You know what? Don't bother coming in to clean out your desk this time. I'll place your things outside in a box. You can find them by the trash hopper. Right next to Reed's junk!"

He turned to leave and stepped right into Mr. Sheppard. Her dad looked like he was ready to tear Trey apart limb by limb. The older man growled. "Get away from my girls. I think it's time for you to go, Mr. Brubaker... or maybe I should help you leave."

Rose called out, "Trey, wait."

But Trey was a man on a mission. He stepped around Rose's father. "Don't bother yourself. I can find my own way out. Thanks for nothing—all of you. Goodbye, Rose Sheppard... and good riddance."

Chapter Twenty-three

Selena's head rested on the pillow, but she knew sleep wasn't coming. She was waiting for the storm to arrive—one named Trey.

Rose had called to let Selena know what happened between her and Trey. Shortly afterwards, Reed phoned to warn her about Trey's foul mood. One that resulted in Reed's bloody nose. Before Trey left Lancaster, he told Reed that Selena was next on his list.

Straining to pick up the slightest noise from outside, Selena recalled the conversation with Rose.

"I told Trey it was over."

"How did he react?"

"He was quite angry."

"At who?"

"Though I told Trey that Reed wasn't involved, he jumped to that conclusion. He also questioned me about the walk you and I had on the beach. I'm afraid he thinks you two had something to do with this."

"Did you tell him about your vision?"

"Only that Trey wasn't the man God planned for me."

"Please tell me you didn't share the rest of your vision with him."

"I promise, I didn't."

The throb of an engine interrupted the stillness of the evening. The motor continued to idle, disturbing the peace of the quiet countryside. Selena knew Trey had finally arrived. Immediately after Reed's call, Selena had phoned Beth. The Warrens had come over and insisted on staying the night at Selena's house, in the room next to hers.

Dropping her cell into a pocket, she grasped the large Mag-light from the bedside table. It would make a good weapon if it came down to it. As soon as she opened her bedroom door, Selena found Beth and Anderson Warren waiting for her in the hall.

Beth looked terrified. "I heard noises. Is that him outside?"

Selena answered, "I think so."

"Let's call 911 and let the police handle it."

"No. Trey wouldn't hurt me."

Andy touched her arm. "Let me talk to him, first. I can protect you."

"Thanks, but I can't allow that. I appreciate both of you being here. However, Trey is my problem."

With the young married couple following mere inches behind her, Selena led the way to the front door. She had expected to find Trey banging her door down, but so far, nothing. Peering into the night, Selena quickly located Trey. He was sitting on the hood of his car, knees drawn up and head down.

Beth whispered in her ear, "What's he doing?"

"Just sitting there."

"Good. Leave him outside. Maybe he'll get the hint and drive away."

That would most likely be the prudent thing to do, but Selena's heart went out to Trey. She could only imagine the pain he felt when Rose broke off their romance. And she knew something else. Trey had seen the same thing she had at the beach—the way Reed had looked at Rose with longing as she slept. No wonder he'd been mad at his best friend. But why was he here? Was he going to try and take his anger out on her? She tightened the grip on the Mag-light.

Trey slid off the car hood and walked in front of the headlamps. Selena unsnapped the deadbolt.

"Selena Harper, what are you doing?" Beth's harsh whisper filled the silence of the house.

"I can't let him stand out there all alone."

Andy touched her arm. "Better out there than in here. Didn't you say he hit Reed?"

"Trey has to be feeling miserable."

Beth pleaded with her. "I bet Reed is as well. Please, don't leave the house."

Selena grasped the doorknob and twisted it. "I have to go."

"You're acting crazy. Why would you even consider facing Trey when he might be dangerous?"

She knew Beth wouldn't understand. "Because once upon a time, I loved him."

***

The commotion from downstairs woke Rose. Her father's raised voice was countered by another one, which sounded calm, yet pleading with the man.

"Mr. Sheppard, I just need to know Rose is all right. If I can just see her for a moment, I'll leave. I know she and Trey broke up and…"

Recognizing the voice, Rose slipped a housecoat over her shoulders. When she opened her door, Lily was standing at the top of the stairs. She appeared to have been waiting on Rose. "Are you okay?"

"I'm fine."

"Is that Reed downstairs?"

"Yes."

"Why would he be here? Did you call him and tell him you broke up with Trey?"

Rose shook her head.

"Then how would he know?"

"I'm not sure, but I'm going to find out."

Walking down the stairs, Rose felt as if she were beginning a new chapter in her life. Her father stood in the opening of the front door, blocking the man she knew was waiting out there. Was her true destiny really waiting for her? In her heart, Rose hoped she knew why Reed had come.

"Look, young man, it's almost eleven o'clock. I am not waking my daughter up for you or any other man. Whatever you want to say to her can wait until tomorrow."

Her dad jumped when Rose touched his arm. "It's okay, Daddy. This is my friend, Reed. I need to speak with him."

Her father studied her face before stepping back. "Okay, Rose. But know this, I'm going to be waiting—right here. It's late."

Rose nodded. "I know. Daddy, I know. We won't be long. I promise."

Casting a glance at her friend, she was taken back. His shirt had dark stains she knew were blood. His left eye was black and blue. Dried, crusty material was in his beard. "I'm sorry to bother you, Rose. But Trey was in a horrible mood. He told me the two of you broke up, and he blames Selena and I for causing it. He said Selena was next on his list, but I couldn't go to help her. Not before I saw you. I needed to make sure he didn't hurt you. Please tell me you're okay. That's all I want to know."

She was touched. Reed had to be in pain, but he drove over to make sure she was fine. "I'm much better... now. Let me get you a cool cloth for your eye and then we can sit on the swing."

He held his hands in front of him, but she noticed they were trembling. "You don't have to. I just wanted to see in person that you were all right. The hour's late and I can go now."

"Nonsense. Please sit down. I'll be right there."

His breath was ragged. "Well, okay."

Rose headed for the door, only to have it swing open. Lily stood there, a small tray in her hands. It held a small bag of crushed ice, a tea towel, some wet paper towels and two glasses of tea. Right away, Rose knew her family would be listening in on their conversation. *Good. This will be a shock, but I want them to hear this.*

She thanked her twin and returned to Reed. Setting down the tray, she gently wiped the mess from his face.

"You don't need to do this."

"If the roles were reversed, this would be you, helping me."

"I'd like to think so, but that's different."

Rose offered a smile she hoped was encouraging. "Uh-huh. You've always been there when I needed you."

"I have?"

"Um-hmm. Remember that day when you found me at Longwood? I desperately needed a friend, and look what God sent me—my *best* friend."

He swallowed hard. "I never should have read that note. I had no right. I'm sorry."

"But you did, and actually, you did have a right to look at it. And then when I was drowning, you were the one who found me. If not for you, I wouldn't be alive."

"But it was Selena who knew what to do."

"Yes, but we're not talking about her. My eyes were opened that day, and it was as if I saw you for the first time. Ever since we met, you've always been there for me, as if your steps were directed by the Lord. You memorized everything I ever shared with you. Why was that?"

His response was slow. "Because you're my friend."

She wrapped the towel around the bag of ice and gently held it to his bruised eye. "That you have been and hopefully always will be. But this is a new day and my heart is open to you, Reed. We can speak the truth, plainly and openly with each other from now on. As I look back in time, it's quite obvious. You've felt more than friendship all along, haven't you?"

Reed bit his lips as he took her in with his single unimpaired eye. "Am I that easy to read?"

"Yes. Guess what? You don't have to hide it anymore. The two of us, we can be honest with each other from now on. Now tell me, over the years, what have I been missing?"

His single eye swept back and forth between hers. "Love. I can't help it. I've been in love with you since the first time I saw you. But you were so focused on Trey, and I, I couldn't say anything. Your happiness was more important to me than my own. I knew your heart belonged to Trey Brubaker."

Rose suddenly saw Reed in a whole new light. She touched his unblemished cheek. "It doesn't anymore. It's yours now." Boldness filled her heart and she leaned forward. Reed met her halfway and their lips blended together. Reed held her tightly in his arms and she could picture God showering her with armfuls of blessings from Heaven. From inside the house, she heard the laughter and cheers of both Lily and her mother. And Rose no longer cared who knew. She was holding the one—and only—man God had created for her.

The alert for a text message on his cell interrupted the moment. Reed backed away, smiling at Rose. But when he extracted the phone from his pocket, the smile disappeared and his face blanched.

Rose knew something was wrong. "What is it?"

"The text is from Trey. It reads, 'Please help me! This is an emergency!!! Call me immediately, please?' That man has got a lot of nerve. First, he punches me, then fires me, and now he wants me to help him? I don't know if I have the energy to speak to him ever again."

Reed's eyes met hers. Rose squeezed his hands. "Then draw your strength from me. Let's call him, together."

***

Selena stepped into the cool night air. From her vantage point, she could see the man's silhouette. He was standing on the far side of his car and appeared to be facing away from her. Moving closer, Selena called to him, "Trey, is everything all right?"

His voice was softer than she expected. "No, it's not."

"Want to talk?"

"I'm surprised you would even give me the time of day."

She walked past the beams of light from the auto lamps until she was by his side. "What's going on?"

"I got my payback."

"What?"

"For all those years ago—when I threw us away. For what I did to you."

"I don't understand what you're saying."

He finally turned to face her. In the dim light from the headlight's reflections, she could almost make out his features. He was upset. "You know, when I broke up with you years ago, I only considered my feelings, not yours. I failed to think of how much pain I caused you."

"Trey, all that's in the past."

He didn't seem to hear her. "Well tonight, Rose dumped me. And I see the similarities. Neither of us did anything wrong to provoke the split. And for the first time, I really get it."

"What do you understand?"

"What I did to you. How badly this breakup hurts. I feel like my heart has been ripped from my chest, thrown to the floor and run over by a herd of buffalo." He sought her eyes. "I loved Rose." Trey paused. "Like you used to love me." He stopped and stared off into the night for a while before continuing.

Selena didn't interrupt, waiting for him to continue.

"One thing I've come to realize... all I do is hurt those close to me. I drove you away. And tonight? I made a grand fool of myself at Rose's house... in front of her family. Then I got into an argument with my best friend and left him standing there bleeding. And then I fired both Reed and Rose."

"Oh, Trey..."

"Then I drove up here with the full intent of telling you off. I just knew you had something to do with the whole enchilada."

"But I didn't."

The man's head was down and he used his foot to dig at something on the ground. "I understand that now. I had plenty of time to think about a lot of different things on the drive up here. And I came to a realization."

"Which is?"

Trey exhaled. "I'm the world's biggest fool. I lost my temper with two of the people I care about the most and probably destroyed those relationships forever."

Selena touched his arm. "Reach out and apologize. They'll forgive you."

"I already did call them. I begged both of them not to leave the company." He lifted his eyes to meet hers. "Guess what? When I called Reed, he and Rose were already together."

She could only imagine how that must have hurt. "I'm sorry."

"And it made me realize something. I hurt you all those years ago and never once said I was sorry." He grasped both of her hands, tightly. "Selena, if you have it in your heart, please forgive me. Breaking up with you was the stupidest thing I ever did."

Things were moving too quickly. "Trey…"

The man must have read her thoughts. "I'm not asking for us to pick up where we left off. I know that ship has sailed. I'm only asking for your forgiveness."

She touched his cheek with her hand. "You have it. I forgave you years ago."

"Thank you." He backed away from her. "I decided I'm going away for a while. Would you do me a favor and keep an eye on Reed and Rose for me?"

"Where are you going?"

"Somewhere that is far enough away so I can't hurt the people I love anymore. To a place that's quiet, so I can meditate and decide who I really am… how my life should be."

"You don't need to do that."

His gaze was sad. "Oh, but I do. So once again, I find myself telling you farewell." He briefly hugged her and pulled away. "Until we meet again, my friend. And maybe when you see the brand new me... it will be a man we'll both proud of."

With that, Trey slid into the driver's seat and drove off into the night. Selena's eyes followed the tail lights until they disappeared from view.

She spoke softly now, knowing God could hear her prayers. "Watch over Trey and heal him, Lord. And if You really intended Trey for me, bring him back into my arms."

Chapter Twenty-four

The crackle of the fireplace and the sound of laughter filled the great room. Selena's "family" sat gathered in the glass enclosed observatory the Warrens had built into their home overlooking the fish pond. Beth's family, Andy's grandparents, Selena's grandmother, Lily, Nate, Rose and Reed were all seated around the beautifully decorated tree. They were exchanging gifts. On this Christmas Eve, everyone Selena really cared about was there, except one person.

Rose handed a beautifully wrapped gift to Selena. "I got this, just for you."

Reed readied his phone to capture the moment. "I'm ready. Open it, Selly."

Glancing around the room, Selena sensed everyone knew what was in the package. "Let me give you your gift at the same time."

The pretty blonde laughed and shook her head. "Nope. It's your turn first."

With great care, Selena removed the ribbon and freed the gift box from the paper. Inside was a jeweler's case. Glancing again at Rose, Selena's eyes drifted to the engagement ring on her friend's finger. The one Reed had given her on Thanksgiving.

"Open it."

Lifting the lid, Selena first removed a handwritten note. It read, "To Selena, my friend both in this life and for eternity." Tears of thanksgiving filled her eyes, so she wiped her cheeks with her fingers. Beneath the note was a sterling silver heart.

Rose encouraged her. "Open it up." Inside was a recent photo of the two of them.

"This is gorgeous." Selena placed the chain around her neck. "Thank you."

Rose embraced her and whispered in her ear, "No, thank you. Not just for saving me, but for sharing your life with me. I've never had a friend like you."

Selena returned to her seat between Rose and Beth. Despite the happiness and frivolity that abounded in this gathering, something was missing.

"Look," Grandma Belinda exclaimed. "It's snowing!" All eyes took in the beauty of the falling snow.

As the afternoon progressed, something tugged at Selena's heartstrings. No one had heard a word from Trey since he drove off that night. And somewhere in this universe, she knew he sat alone. *Please watch over him, Lord. Let him know he is loved, needed and wanted.*

"How about some warm apple cider?"

She found Beth standing there, interrupting her pity party. When Beth saw Selena's face, her friend's expression changed and her lifelong friend opened her arms. "There, there. It will be fine."

"I miss him."

"I know."

"I was kind of hoping he would show up, but I guess that was a dumb wish."

"It's still early. Who knows? Maybe a Christmas miracle will happen. Just believe. After all, it's in God's time, not ours."

Selena looked away. *Please keep him safe, Lord. And if You are willing, please bring him back to me.*

Since the snow was beginning to accumulate, the Lancaster visitors left early. It would be a slow and potentially hazardous trip back on snowy roads.

Despite their best efforts, the comfort and closeness of Beth's family exacerbated the hole in her heart. It was well after eleven when she stood and hugged Beth.

"I guess I should be going."

"Nonsense."

"Christmas is a time to celebrate with your family."

"We are your family."

"I know, but..."

"Please stay."

"Thanks, but I'm going home."

Beth smoothed Selena's hair. "Then I'll drive you."

"No, I need to clear my head. The walk will do me good, and besides, it's just across the road."

"Fine, go ahead and freeze to death. I know where I'm not wanted."

"Silly, this is your house. I'm simply returning to mine."

Selena buttoned her coat and Beth wrapped a scarf around Selena's neck. "Breakfast is at eight, but come over anytime you want... before breakfast preferably."

"Okay. 'Night and Merry Christmas."

Outside, the snow was really coming down. Selena could no longer make out the tire tracks from the vehicles that had left earlier. She had just rounded the last bend when something wet struck her forehead. Was it a pile of snow from an overhead branch—or had it been a snowball?

Selena stopped and searched the trees along the lane. She didn't see anything out of place. Continuing, barely two steps had gone by when another wad of snow smacked against her chest. Again, she surveyed the trees. Nothing, but now she knew someone was out there.

With a braveness she didn't really feel, Selena called out, "I know you're there. Show yourself before I come looking for you."

Movement in the pines twenty feet to her left drew her attention. A man emerged from the tree line. A chill ran down her spine.

"Merry Christmas, Selena."

Despite the cold, her whole body warmed. "Trey?"

A man she didn't fully recognize until he stood five feet from her emerged from the dark. "Remember how we loved to walk together in the snow? And those snowball fights we used to have?"

Selena stepped forward and touched his face. "Is it really you?"

"Yes."

"Why are you here?"

"Well, it is Christmas. A time you should spend with the ones you love."

They simply stared at each other. He broke the silence. "It's really cold. I've been waiting outside for hours so I could walk you home. Can we go in where it's warm?"

"Of course."

After they entered Selena's house and took off their snowy cloaks, Selena put a pot of water on the stove for tea. Turning, she studied the man sitting in her kitchen. He looked different. His hair was almost as long as hers and his beard was littered with flecks of grey hair. But Trey's eyes hadn't changed.

"I haven't heard from you for months, and now you show up? Are you okay?"

Trey nodded. "I'm done with soul searching. Everything is like crystal to me now."

"What's clear?"

"My destiny. My purpose in life."

His eyes sparkled in the glow of the kitchen lights.

"And what did you find?"

He laughed. "That my future depends... on you."

It was very hot in the kitchen. "On me? Why?"

"It depends on whether you'll give me another chance. Selena, I really believe you and I were meant to be. I was too stupid to realize it when we were kids." He stood and touched her face. "I lost you once, and I want to win you back, if you'll let me try. If you say no, I'll leave—right now. But if you can give me a single chance, I promise, I'll make you happier than you ever dreamed possible. Shall I stay?"

Selena kissed his fingers. "Yes. I want that, too."

Trey wrapped his arms around her. "Do you think we have a shot?"

"I believe so with all my heart."

The warmth of his breath against her cheek thrilled her. "Even after all that happened?"

"Yes. Do you know why?"

"No."

"Do you remember Rose's vision—the one God sent her?"

Trey paled and he released her. "Y-yes. The one where she said I wasn't meant for her."

Selena could barely contain her smile as she drew him close. "She didn't tell you the last part."

"What was it?"

"In her dream, God told Rose that she had to let you go… because the good Lord made you for me, not her." His mouth dropped open. Selena took his hands and drew him close.

Their lips met just as her grandfather clock rang out midnight. Selena sent a message to Heaven as she held him, *Thank You, God, for answering my prayers.*

Epilogue

The day was bright and sunny, without a single cloud in the sky. The Sheppards' backyard had been transformed into a dreamland full of tulle, lace and of course, flowers.

In Rose's room, Lily and Selena were fussing over the final touches to Rose's gown. Selena had never seen Lily as ecstatic, and Rose? A puff of air could blow her over.

Mr. Sheppard knocked before sticking his head in the door. "Five minutes before I walk you down the aisle, Rose. Are you ready?"

The girl's appearance was exquisite. "Yes, Daddy. I'll be down in a jiffy."

After he left, Rose's mother appeared and opened a box containing a piece of jewelry. "Rose, this is a broach my great-grandmother gave my grandmother on her wedding day. It has been passed down the line to the eldest daughter in the family. And today, I'm giving it to you." Her mom pinned it on her dress, kissed her daughter's cheek and descended the stairs.

Selena noted the look of sadness on Lily's face. Rose must have seen it too, because she touched her sister's hand and turned Lily toward her. "We're the first twins in the family, Lily. We're going to break tradition. You and I will share this broach. When you marry, I'll pin it on your gown. So, let's make a new pact. This pin will be worn by each of our daughters on their wedding days, okay?"

The younger girl's face visibly brightened. "Thank you. Now, if you'll excuse me, I need to use the restroom before it all starts."

As soon as Lily departed, Rose smiled at Selena. "Do you remember the walk on the beach in Rehoboth? When I told you about the vision I had?"

"Yes."

"It continues to come true. You're in my wedding today."

Selena smiled. "And you'll be in mine next month."

Rose's eyes became shiny. "I can't wait."

"If someone would have told me a year ago that things would turn out this way, I never would have believed them. That you would marry Reed and me... becoming Trey's wife. Quite a story we'll pass on to our children."

Rose squeezed her hand. "But Someone already told us this tale. It's funny how God speaks to us."

"Yeah, it is."

"And this is just the beginning. You, Selena Harper, soon to be Brubaker, are stuck with me for all eternity. Just think... joint vacations, family visits, holding each other's babies..."

Selena held up her hands. "Slow down on that baby thing, girl. Trey and I aren't even married yet."

Rose giggled. "Well, that was the next thing in the vision."

It was Selena's turn to laugh. "Then let's play it in slow motion."

***

The reception was winding down. Reed and his bride had changed out of tux and gown and were saying their final goodbyes to the parents. Selena and Trey waited in the Subaru. They were driving the newlyweds to the airport hotel. The Thomases were heading off to Hawaii for a seventeen-day honeymoon. Since Selena had lived in the island state, she had planned the itinerary and Trey had footed the bill.

Finally, Reed held the door open for his bride and then climbed in after her.

Selena's smile had to be a mile wide, full of happiness for her friends. "Are you finally ready to begin your life together?"

The couple could only answer, "Um-hmm." That was because they were embracing. Again.

After what felt like an eternity, Rose said, "Thanks again for this gift. It is more than generous."

Trey had a smile on his face. "I can't think of two people who deserve it more... except maybe Selena and I." She caught the wink he sent her way. "I can let you know now, Rose, since the ceremony is over and such... Reed and I had this agreement. You see, I'm paying for your trip and he's footing ours. All *three weeks* of it."

The new husband guffawed. "That's right. A glamorous twenty-one-night stay at, get this, the luxurious Motel Six right here in Lancaster."

The car was full of laughter, but Trey's was loudest. "Oh, I see how it goes. We provide the fare to an exotic location and you send us to the land of horse-drawn buggies and strip malls."

"I don't see what the big deal is," Reed somehow managed to get out. "I mean, we're honeymooners. Do we even have to leave the hotel room?"

Rose tapped her man on the arm. "Ignore him. My husband is cheap when he's footing the bill, but no luxury is too great if somebody else is writing the check. Did you know when we were planning the reception dinner, Reed told my parents the meal should be surf and turf?"

Reed gave it right back to her. "And your dad said, 'That's perfect. Fish sticks and hot dogs is fine by me.' They say girls marry someone like their dad..."

Selena joined in. "So, you're saying your cheapness is what attracted Rose to you?"

Rose took a shot. "There were other factors, but that kind of topped them."

A few minutes later, Trey commented, "You know, I'm glad God created forgiveness and that each one of you had it in your heart to give me another chance. Everything was really going downhill there for a while."

The bride was the one who answered. "God never promised life would be easy. His oath was that He'd never forsake us."

"Well, thank you all anyway." The man's voice was teasing when he added, "Of course, some of us had an advantage. You know, getting to read the script ahead of time."

Selena now joined in. "Well, I for one am glad Rose did have that vision. Poor girl, she could have been stuck with you."

She could feel her fiancé's eyes on her. "That wouldn't have happened."

"Really? Why do you say that?"

"Because, Selena, long before Heaven and earth were formed, He intended us for each other. And I'm glad He did."

"Me, too."

Trey leaned across the seat to kiss her cheek. "I guess true love does win out."

Selena laughed. "That's right. Know why?"

He shook his head.

She couldn't help but smile. "Because God decreed you were, you are, and always will be my destiny."

Want to see where it all started?

**If you liked *Destiny*,
you'll love these...**

Treasure in Paradise

While researching characters for her upcoming book, Jasmine finds a real doozy in Josh Miller, a highly talented man who is doing his best to keep his skills hidden. Jasmine knows he's hiding something, so she keeps digging into Josh's life. Who knows? If she mines deep enough, she might find treasure.

Scan this QR code to order *Treasure in Paradise*, Christian Journeys in Paradise, Book 7.

paperback

large print

Road to Paradise

Beth may be young, but she knows what she wants – a once-in-a-lifetime fairytale romance. After her first date with Anderson Warren, she believes she's met Prince Charming. But when his ex-fiancée storms into town like a tornado and leaves a swath of destruction between them, is there any way to put in back together?

Scan this QR code to order *Road to Paradise,* a Paradise Sweetheart Romance Novella.

Autumn in Paradise

Everything Annie worked for is gone. After losing both her job and boyfriend, she moves to Lancaster to start over. She soon finds herself in the company of two men. One is her mind's perfect choice, yet the other pulls at her heartstrings. Which should she follow – her mind or her heart? Scan this QR code to order *Autumn in Paradise*, Christian Journeys in Paradise, Book 8.

paperback   *large print*

West of Paradise

After three failed marriages, Teresa believes true love isn't on the menu. Until she meets red-bearded, ex-sea captain AJ Showers. It seems the man's mission is to make her life a wonderful dream. But when Teresa discovers the secret that AJ and the young neighbor woman share, will their romance sink... or will they sail off into the sunset happily ever after?

Scan this QR code to order *West of Paradise,* a Paradise Sweetheart Romance Novella.

Want to read more of Chas's books?

*Get **Skating in Paradise** free when you subscribe to the newsletter.*

Visit www.ChasWilliamson.com to claim your free book!

Every day is a struggle for oncology nurse Tammy Kunkle. After cancer took both her little girl and husband, she's dedicated her life solely to helping others. But when she visits a former child patient, she's introduced to a man filled with a warm, faithful spirit. Could it be Tammy has met her new future?

Download your free copy of *Skating in Paradise* today.

www.chaswilliamson.com

Did you like *Destiny*?
Please consider leaving a review for other readers.

For a complete list of Chas's books visit
www.ChasWilliamson.com

Dedication

To Janet

Destiny is a story of transformation. For our heroine, everything that once was solid, steady and normal is past.

This book is dedicated to the woman who helped me transform my childhood life into *our* future, one exponentially better than I ever dreamed possible.

I'm not a bright man. To help me, the first time I saw you, Janet, God seemed to light your face with a spotlight. That was all it took and like a match to dry kindling, my heart was ablaze for you.

Now, pushing half a century later, I find myself falling deeper and deeper in love with you each and every day. When I think about our triumphs, failures, highs and lows, I'm glad my life was entwined with yours. And still, hand-in-hand, we stroll toward eternity together. You are my world and will be forever.

This book, and my life, are dedicated to you, Janet.

True love lasts forever!

Acknowledgments

To God, for bringing the right people into our lives just when we need them.

To Janet, my favorite person. You are the light of my life, my inspiration, my joy, my world.

To Demi, editor, publisher and friend. Thank you for helping my dreams come true. Without you, my characters would simply be unrealized figments of my imagination.

To the beta reading team of Janet, Sarah, Connie, Mary, Bekah and Diane and for their assistance and guidance as we now journey to *South Mountain*.

To my children, the joy of my heart, and my grandchildren, the jewels on my life crown.

To the three who will shape our future. Be not content with the ways of the world, but flavor it with your joy. Never be afraid to show your faith and be *'the salt of the earth'*. Remember Mimi and I will always be with you, in your heart if not by your side.

To my fans. My wish is that God uses the words He placed in my heart to touch and bless your lives. Thank you for being a fan!

To the angels who walk among us. With a purposeful smile, words of encouragement or comforting presence, you change the world and give us all a brief glimpse of Heaven.

About the Author

Chas Williamson's lifelong dream was to write. He started writing his first book at age eight, but quit after two paragraphs. Yet some dreams never fade...

It's said one should write what one knows best. That left two choices—the world of environmental health and safety... or romance. Chas and his bride have built a fairytale life of love. At her encouragement, he began writing romance. The characters you'll meet in his books are very real to him, and he hopes they'll become just as real to you.

True Love Lasts Forever!

Follow Chas on www.bookbub.com

Check out our website at
ChasWilliamson.com

Check us out on Facebook at
Chas Williamson Books

Follow us on Instagram at
Chas Williamson

Made in the USA
Columbia, SC
08 June 2024